FLY
WITH ME

Fly With Me

Cover Design by The Book Brander
TheBookBrander.com
Content Edits: Sue Brown-Moore
SueBrownMoore.com
Copy Edits: Danielle Fine
DanielleFine.com
Print Formatting by Nina Pierce of Seaside Publications
NinaPierce.com/book-formatting/

First Edition
ISBN: 979-8-9867802-3-8

FLY WITH ME

SILVERSTAR MATES

INTERGALACTIC DATING AGENCY

USA TODAY BESTSELLING AUTHOR

LEA KIRK

SFR by LEA KIRK

The Prophecy Series
(in chronological order)

Prophecy
Book One

Blue Christmas
A Prophecy Series Holiday Novella

Space Ranger
A Prophecy Series Short Story
(*newsletter exclusive*)

All of Me
A Prophecy Series Short Story

Salvation
Book Two

Collision
Book Three

Skylar's Gift
A Prophecy Series Novella

Paradox
(Coming Soon)

Silverstar Mates Series
(in recommended reading order)

Fly With Me
Above the Storm
Wing and a Prayer
Trial by Fire

PNR by LEA KIRK

Made for Her
Part of S. E. Smith's, The Worlds of Magic, New Mexico

ONE

———✴———

Present day.

"For Chrissake, Regina, what kind of aliens abduct a sixty-year-old woman?" The helpless frustration at her predicament boiled up in Ava Marie Martin's gut again as she stalked a perimeter wall of the gleaming white cell. "In her hair rollers, no less."

The hair rollers in question bounced against her thighs inside the overstuffed pockets of her silk bathrobe.

She turned to retrace her steps. "I'll tell you who. Blind aliens, that's who."

And I made it so easy for them, didn't I?

Walked right into their trap then poof, one flash of green light later, here she was, like an extra from Close Encounters. A bunch of stereotypical Area 51 regulars, the lot of them, with their putty-tone skin and freaky monochromatic eyes.

Guess I'm a believer now.

Couldn't really be a skeptic since she'd become one of

those people. The ones at whom she used to shake her head and roll her eyes. God Almighty.

The less-than-satisfying pat-pat-pat of her bedroom slippers against the black porous floor wasn't helping ease her current fit of temper, either. What she'd give for a pair of spikey, angry shoes and a solid metal floor right now.

"Cha, honey," Regina said from his spot on the floor, somehow still looking fantastic in his vinyl, school-bus yellow mini-skirt and thigh-high boots, even after a week in captivity. "You're as stuck as the rest of us."

Her cellmate had that right. "I know, and it still pisses me off."

There hadn't been a single clue that "Motel Stardust" was actually a spaceship in disguise—parked neatly at the edge of a cracked asphalt parking lot. Who asked questions like that when driving a dark Nevada highway, a hundred miles from Vegas in the middle of the night, anyway? Not her. Obviously.

"Why? Wait, don't answer that." Regina—aka, Reg "Don't Call Me Reginald" Gardenia—waved one manicured hand in the air like the drag queen he was in his Vegas revue. "It's because you have no control over the situation. Am I right?"

She came to a stop directly across the ten-foot cell from Reg, the edges of her silk robe fluttering like bird's wings around her matching cornflower-blue PJs. Control was at the crux of it all, as it had been for most of her life. She'd worn it like a shield, even when she was quaking in her boots. It'd been her constant companion, facing situations from ridicule and abandonment by certain family members for daring to stand up for herself, to building her multi-million-dollar cosmetics company.

"Okay. You might be right."

"You know I am." Reg nodded as if satisfied with this level of recognition. "We've gone over this before. Being pissed isn't going to do you any good. It's been at least a week, darling. Time to let it go."

"Let her be, Regina." The gentle voice came from the young woman in the second, larger cell across a wide walkway. "There's no set timeframe for going through the stages of grief."

Huh. She frowned and drew her eyebrows together. Leave it to Nora the Wicked-smart Librarian to figure out she'd been following the parameters of grieving, almost exactly. The young woman had a sense of awareness that would've made her an outstanding personal assistant.

Not that I need one of those anymore.

No, she'd sold her business, waved good-bye to her staff, and driven off into the proverbial sunset to retire and enjoy her "golden years." Yeah, that plan was working out just swell.

"Well, if I ever turn into a raging Mama Bear like Ava is now, just bitch-slap me back to reality, okay?"

Nora snorted. "Reality equals boredom in here. Nothing to do, and no books to read."

Poor kid did look thoroughly bored lying on her back, head propped on the thigh of her buff stud-muffin cellmate.

"Mooo."

The human one, not the bovine. Call that rumor confirmed. Not only did aliens exist, they also really did abduct cows.

"Sorry, May Belle," Nora said to the large, straw-color beast nosing at her sandy blonde hair. "You're not boring, sweetie."

The young man gazed down at Nora and cleared his throat in a pointed manner.

"Neither are you, Axill." She patted the muscular forearm resting across her belly.

"Takk," Axill replied in his native Norwegian then grinned.

Was there a more unlikely pair than those two? The hot, blond actor who played some Norse god from the Cosmos Warriors movies, and the librarian who looked an awful lot like Velma from Scooby-Doo.

"Thor is definitely not boring," Regina teased.

"I do not play Thor," Axill grumbled.

"Cha, darling boy. I know." Regina flashed a teasing grin, his teeth as white against his brown skin as his cotton-blonde Dolly Parton wig.

Nora turned her head to peer at Regina through both sets of light bars holding them inside their respective cells. "He plays Týr, a god originally from Germanic mythology and likely the source of the word Tuesday."

You can take the girl out of the library, but you can't take the librarian out of the girl.

"I know, but it's all about perspective. And in my perspective, I couldn't care less about which god Axill Lund portrays on screen, I'd still pay to watch him."

Nora's giggle floated from across the cell, and the corners of Axill's mouth twitched upward. Okay, so maybe all of them had bonded to some degree. There was some sort of psychology about that, wasn't there?

She stepped toward the glowing yellow bars of light—not too close, because their shock packed a brain-numbing punch—to study the couple in the other cell. "So, Nora was grabbed leaving her library job at two in the morning, and I got suckered into a fake motel. What about you, Axill?"

The muscular hunk shrugged his wide shoulders. "Between movies, I like to spend time at my cabin outside of Eidfjord. It is remote, no neighbors for a long way. One night, I hear a loud noise, so I go check. It was them."

"That sounds like a more classic abduction scenario. Still, I'm sorry you're here." Sorry any of them were.

"Me too." Reg stretched his long legs straight out then tugged the tops of his boots into place. "Not that I regret meeting any of you, but getting abducted was a sucky way to end my otherwise fabulous evening."

She eyed her cellmate. "Are you finally ready to tell us what happened to you?"

"Sure, why not? I'm over most of the humiliation at this point. Especially after hearing all of y'all's stories." Reg folded his hands in his lap. "So, I was on my way back from a cast party and thought I'd found a new pop-up convenience store outside of town. One moment, I had my head in the freezer hunting for a pint of Banana Hammock flavor ice-cream, the next I was in this cell thinking da faq? Actually, I may have screamed that."

"You did." Rather loudly, in fact.

It had been Regina's voice that'd pulled her out of her own vacuum of shock brought on by this nightmare.

"Mooo." May Belle ambled away to the farthest wall from her two people, then proceeded to relieve herself.

5

"Huh," Nora said. "I didn't think it'd work, but she's getting pretty good at that."

"So, Nora Weber," Reg said in a deeper-than-normal voice. "You were abducted by a UFO, thrown into an alien jail, and traveled to untoward parts of the galaxy that no Earthling has visited. What was your biggest accomplishment while you were in space?" He schooled his face into a parody of Nora's shy smile. "I potty trained a cow."

A little snicker bubbled out of Ava before she could catch it, but it was lost in the raucous laughter coming from Nora and Axill.

"Thanks, Regina." Nora was sitting up now, her legs crisscrossed. She waved her hand in the direction of May Belle's contribution to the floor. "All I can say is that these last couple of weeks would've been a lot worse if not for the waste-absorbent floor in here."

"Ja. Or, if our cell was as small as Regina and Ava's," Axill added.

That much was true. Having to pop a squat with no privacy was bad enough, but at least the waste didn't sit around. One of the first things she and Reg had done after waking up in here was to agree on a designated corner to do their business.

A sense of mild morose settled over her. Damn mood swings. She trudged over and claimed a spot against the wall next to Reg. She should've been in Vegas with the girls right now, gambling, going to shows, picking up guys...*celebrating* her stinking retirement. Amazing how fast a year of planning with her besties had gone to hell.

The girls must have reported her missing by now. At the very least, someone should've found her car sitting in the middle of the desert. What a shame she couldn't hand that little convertible over to Robyn like she'd planned. All the work she'd done investigating how to legally sign it over to her niece—keeping Robyn's piece-of-shit husband's name off the title—wasted. But none of that mattered anymore.

Oh, my poor sweet Robyn.

A sound somewhere between a soft chuckle and a scoff escaped her.

"What's up, honey?"

She raised her gaze and met Regina's. "What do you suppose gray-haired old me has in common with any of you youngsters?"

That caught Nora's attention. The little bespectacled librarian moved to stand by the light bars of her cell. "You mean, what do four humans and a cow have in common?"

"Yes." The cow who was now receiving an ear scratch from Axill. "What kind of cow is May Belle, anyway?"

"Mooo."

"Hmm." Nora cast a critical eye at the creature. "She might be a Charolais, or maybe a Murray Grey."

"Charolais," Axill said as the cow tipped her head into his palm and closed her eyes halfway.

Regina frowned. "And how does a Norwegian actor happen to know anything about cow breeds, or whatever it's called?"

Axill looked up, gave him a small smile, then returned his attention to the cow in question.

Silence fell over their little cellblock, as if everyone had retreated into their own personal thoughts. She pinched a strand of her chin-length hair and twirled it around one finger. Gray, white, off-white, two blond—

"Hey," Reg murmured. "Still feeling pissed?"

"Not so much, for the moment." She lifted the silvery lock far enough to give it a critical eye. "But I think I just answered my own question. All of us have light color hair. Including the cow."

"Ha! Not under my wig, I don't."

"True, but do the aliens know that?" She raised her shoulders in a nonchalant shrug.

Nora hummed. "That's interesting. We all have some variant of light color hair."

"Well." Regina huffed and touched his fingers to his wig. "If that *is* the reason we were taken, someone's going to be mighty surprised by me."

"Mooo?"

A shudder rumbled through the floor under Ava's bottom, and she snapped her gaze to Regina's. "Did you feel that?"

"Yeah." Regina's wide eyes reflected surprised uncertainty, similar to feeling the first jolt of an earthquake.

Another, harder tremble shook the walls.

She scrambled to her knees and met Nora's startled gaze through the bars. "Has that ever happened before?"

"No."

A high-pitched whine, like over-taxed engines, filled the cellblock and the room began to tilt.

I have a bad feeling about this.

"Hang on!" Axill's bellow was barely audible over the mechanical screeching, but it was enough to jar her senses back into place.

Hang on to what? She turned her head in quick, jerky movements, scanning the smooth white walls for anything to grab on to, but there was nothing. The floor was a pliable, non-slippery matte material, though.

"Reg, lie flat and try to dig in with your fingernails." She lurched forward, landing belly first on the floor, and her cellmate mimicked her movement by her side.

Everything kept tilting up and up and up, sending her half sliding, half falling toward the dreaded shock bars.

"No, no, no, no." She clawed at the floor, trying to get a grip with her fingers, toes, or heels as she rolled.

A cold sweat broke out over her top lip and her heart pounded against her chest, as if ready to bail on her in an effort to save itself. Just like it did every time she was faced with heights. She caught a flash of bright yellow vinyl and dark flailing limbs, an out-of-control Regina following her silk-covered ass toward the stun-you-stupid bars.

Crap. This is gonna hurt.

TWO

Sovah Raptorclaw stepped through his ready-room doorway and soaked in the calming beeps, chirps, and low murmur of conversation on the bridge. Forty sun migrations, and it had come to this: his final cruise as captain of *Axiom*. He allowed his gaze to travel over his flight crew—his *family*, his flock, in place of the personal one he had never had. By choice. They were a well-meshed crew, as they should be. Worked together seamlessly to protect the upstanding civilians of the Galactic Alliance of Planets from the lawless.

My legacy, really.

There, he was doing it again—heading into the sentimental skies of reminiscing. He gave himself a mental shake, fluffed his wings, then strode toward the captain's perch. The bittersweet ache of nostalgia slid away to lurk in some dark corner until the next time he let his guard down for a poignant moment.

Retirement was a natural progression of life, not the end of it. Certainly not the end of *his* life. Or his career, for that matter. Chief Commissioner Strauss Landwalker had already hinted at an opportunity to join Protectorship Command, a position of honor for a life of service.

And his crew? He paused next to the captain's perch and shifted his gaze to his first officer as she slowly strolled the bridge, overseeing and observing as was her habit. Yes, they would soar under Rota's leadership.

Rota turned her head as if sensing his gaze, and he ran his hand over the cushioned seat of the captain's perch, caressing the deep-blue *vava*-skin, smooth and cool under his taloned fingers. His perch for the past thirty-three sun migrations.

"Are you ready for this, Deputy Captain?" No doubt she could see the teasing grin he was trying to suppress.

Across the bridge, Deputy Captain Rota Raptorclaw inclined her head, her gold and black headfeathers shimmering under the bridge lighting. "If I am not, the fault is my own, Captain. But yes, I am prepared to relieve you upon our return to Bezchi."

"I am not prepared at all." Not at the moment, anyway. But he *should* be, especially since he would be leaving his vessel and his crew under Rota's capable wing-span. "However, I will be ready to hand over *Axiom*'s perch by the time we arrive home."

He released his full grin and slid onto the perch, tucking his wings to keep his balance. Rota chuckled then resumed her stroll.

"Warden First Class Tiya." He turned his attention to the young female at the helm. "Report."

Tiya Landwalker danced her fingers over the controls.

"Not so much as a micro-blip, Captain. The sector is as clear as a cloudless day."

The best days for an easy flight. So far, his final patrol to the edge of Alliance space had been quiet. No run-ins with transgressors of any kind, which was a shame. Quiet was nice, but he had never pictured his space career ending on such an…uninspiring note.

All this inactivity left him with too much time to think about, well, everything. Especially the ever-present misgivings about what it meant to exchange one sort of life for another. Should he accept the new position if Strauss offered it, or devote what was left of his life to being a civilian? Could he spend his days without some sort of structure? Alone?

I have no one to blame but myself about the alone part.

He did not exactly regret the choice he had made as a young male to forgo the Bezchian tradition of having the Firewing elders match him with a mate. A mate who he would have left alone on Bezchi, possibly for up to a full sun migration at a time. It would have been unfair to her. And having an unhappy mate was not an air current upon which he had wished to soar.

Giving a mate fledglings might have helped, but… A small shiver traveled up his spine and through his wings. Even now, the mere thought of fledglings flapping around him made him itch to take wing and escape. Still, many Protectorship officers' mates had found happiness with heirs to distract them. Rota's mate Nyeb kept busy with their three. That was a successful and happy mating for a Protectorship officer.

But that had never been a path for him. Thank the immortals that his own siblings had ensured the continuation of their flock and clan several times over. That was good enough. Besides, it was much easier to visit them, get his fill of the young ones, and then leave. No responsibility to keep and protect his own brood. His crew filled that role in his life. And, as full-grown Bezchians, they were easier to reason with—for the most part.

"Captain." Warden Tiya stiffened on her perch, the scaled gray-blue feathers down the back of her neck rising. "Incoming vessel."

Finally. Something interesting. "Identification?"

"It is one of the grays' vessels, Captain."

A rush of adrenalin coursed through him. More than interesting, it was an opportunity.

Tiya's fingers moved over her consul in a blur. "Cargo class, traveling at high velocity and not slowing."

Because the damn pirates could not detect *Axiom*'s upgraded covert shielding. "Trajectory?"

"They will pass our port bow in thirty wing beats."

Perfect. "Move us into position and deploy the net array."

"Yes, Captain." A faint chime sounded. "Array deployed directly in their path, Captain. They are not diverting."

Sovah gave the younger female a minute nod and turned his attention to the view screen. Precisely thirty wing beats later, the grays' vessel hurdled passed *Axiom*'s port side. It plowed into the invisible array, slowing as the net stretched and stretched until the cargo carrier came to a stop—a barely visible dot of gray on the viewer.

A tremor ran through *Axiom*, and Tiya glanced at him.

"The grays are attempting to break free, Captain."

"Target their propulsion system with a pulse, Warden."

She punched a button and the tremors ceased. "Grays' propulsion system deactivated. Their vessel is wrapped tight. Beginning tow-in now."

A successful apprehension. It was not the grays' bellwether, but every smaller vessel taken out of operation was one less vessel they had to conduct their repugnant trade of illegal goods, including and especially citizens of the Galactic Alliance of Planets.

"Captain, docking tube ready to connect on your order." Tiya wore a smug look of satisfaction on her sandy-brown face.

"Well done, Warden. Alert Sentry Commander Guan Waterdiver to have a boarding party meet me at the docking tube hatchway. Tell him hostiles are expected." He pushed off the captain's perch. "Deputy Captain, hold the bridge."

Rota inclined her head. "Yes, Captain."

Now to find out exactly what cargo the grays carried.

THREE

Voices murmured through the fog blanketing Ava's brain. Muffled, urgent-sounding voices.

"Ava."

Muffled, urgent-sounding voices who somehow knew her name.

"Ava."

She groaned, the sound rattling inside her skull and in every joint, even in her fingers. Bender. She must be coming off a bender...and a weird one, too. There'd been aliens—

"A-*va*!"

"*Whash*?" She forced her eyes open.

Warm moisture seemed to be stuck between her cheek and a familiar black, porous floor. Ew, drool. Must've been one hell of a bender. God Almighty, had she really been that stupid? It'd been three decades since her last one in Cannes, and the tabloids had had a ball painting her as a wild hussy who couldn't keep a man. They never did understand that while men were nice to play with, none of them had ever touched her heart.

"Get up, honey. Are you okay?"

Okay? That was debatable. She drew her arms under her and pushed up, fighting the pins and needles still stabbing at her joints, until she sat upright on the floor.

"Whasha hell happened?" She swiped the back of her hand over her damp cheek—*ick*—then squinted at the dark-complected face hovering close to her own.

Reg. The name attached itself to the face. Then she moved her gaze to the two faces peering at her across a walkway. Through two sets of vertical bars of light. Axill and Nora.

The memories flooded back. Oh, hell…not a bender. Aliens. And every last one of those pricks sucked donkey balls for abducting her. As well as all the others in the cellblock. Then everything had gone haywire, like riding a tilt-a-whirl, sending her straight into the shock bars of her cell, followed by six-feet-two-inches of yellow-clad drag queen.

Which explained *why* she'd been passed out and drooling…on the waste-absorbent floor. So gross. She scrubbed the cuff of her robe sleeve over her cheek again for good measure. Just because she and Reg had used the farthest corner of their cell to do their business, didn't mean prior inmates had.

She squeezed her eyes shut then opened them again. "Fine. I'm fine. You guys?"

"Just peachy." Reg adjusted his cotton-blonde wig until it was straight. "Fuck, those bars hurt."

One of the bars of her and Regina's cell flickered like a spastic strobe. Weird.

Nora tapped a finger against the side of her head. "We're okay over here. The back wall of our cell is pretty hard, but my cranium is harder."

"Mooo." That must've been bovine for "What she said."

A chuckle burbled out. "Well, thank God for that."

"Ava," Nora said. "Something's messing with one of your shock bars."

Huh? She lowered her gaze to the base of the flickering bar. One of her curlers sat smack dab inside it, which shouldn't have been possible because they were solid to the touch.

Reg bent to peer at it. "Looks like it's disrupting the power somehow."

The beam flickered again then blinked out of existence, leaving a gap of about four inches. Dead silence filled the cellblock as realization seeped into her slowly rebooting brain.

She jerked her head up and moved her gaze between Reg and Nora. "Something in the rollers cancels out the beam."

"Maybe the composition of the mesh?" Nora bounced on her toes; her eyes lit with excitement and hope.

Yes. Yes, that could be it! But there was only one way to find out for sure. She shoved her hand into her robe pocket, closed her fingers around one of the largest curlers, and drew it out. The mesh fiber prickled against her palm as she lowered herself belly-down on the floor, her face inches from the shock bars.

"A-vaaa. Be careful, honey." Worry laced Regina's words. "You know what'll happen if you touch them."

"Oh, I've got a pretty good idea." She scooted the roller

along the floor toward an unsuspecting beam with one finger then pushed it as far as she dared through the thing. It flickered but didn't go out. "I need something to push it all the way in."

Regina snorted. "That's what *he* said."

A collective groan came from Nora and Axill.

Ava gave the drag queen a smirk. "Never lose that sense of humor, Reg."

One of her roller clips might work. She drew one out of her pocket, set it against the end of the roller, and applied gentle pressure to nudge it forward. Next to her, Reg sucked air in through his teeth. Then the second shock bar flickered out.

"Ha!" Her shout of triumph echoed through the cellblock, along with her friends' cheers. "Three more ought to be enough to get us out of here."

The process went quickly, and a few minutes later, she and Regina slinked through the opening to freedom. Or, sorta freedom. They still had to figure out how to get off the ship without the gray aliens catching them. That was going to be difficult, but one problem at a time.

She kneeled in front of the shock bars of the other three inmates. "Let's get you guys out of there."

Reg rolled his eyes. "Please tell me we're not taking the cow."

"May Belle," Nora snapped. "And, *yes*, we are."

"Ja, we are," Axill repeated firmly.

That deep voice of his worked as well in real life as it did on the big screen. And the way he backed up Nora without a second thought proved how smitten the huge hunk of

Nordic-god-like man was. The god and the librarian... beyond adorable.

Focus, lady.

There'd be no *them* if they didn't find a way off this ship and back to Earth. This could turn out to be a very short escape, but it beat the hell out of hanging around waiting for destiny. Or doom.

Minutes later, all of them—including May Belle, with Axill leading her by her harness—headed out of the cellblock. There was no door, just an archway into a larger, and eerily empty, passageway.

Reg nibbled his plump lower lip. "Which way, do you think?"

"Hell, if I know." And why were they all looking at her, as if she were the de facto leader of their little group?

It wasn't that any of them were incapable, but apparently, they had unilaterally and without discussion chosen her. She ran her tongue over her lips. An every-person-for-themselves strategy wasn't going to work. Someone would inevitably get left behind, and she'd be damned if she'd abandon any of them like that. Mostly because she knew exactly how *that* felt.

She nodded her head to the left. "Let's try this way."

And with those four words, she accepted the role they'd thrust on her. Could be she'd come to regret it, but she had managed to keep over three decades of employees happy, so how different could this be?

She moved forward with as much confidence as possible, the *pat* of her quilted slippers drowned out by the sharp click of Regina's boots and the clump of cow hooves against the metallic floor. *Now* the floor was metal. Good luck trying to sneak out of here unnoticed.

"Hey!" The voice came from ahead of them. "Who's out there?"

Busted.

She raised her hand to stop the others then pitched her voice to an almost whisper. "Sounds like it came from the archway ahead."

"Other prisoners?" Reg murmured back.

"Could be. Stay here." She padded to the archway ten feet ahead and peered around the corner.

It was another cellblock, and several anxious faces peered out from behind their shock bars as though she were the Second Coming. And not all of them were human, either.

"Christ Almighty." She turned her attention back to her friends. "We gotta go back and get all the hair rollers."

Ava stepped back, and a young, dark-haired kid with two horn nubs sprouting from his head darted out of a cell. He spoke profusely in a language she'd never heard before. But she didn't need to understand; the kid's gratitude was clear.

A smile and a nod seemed to placate him then she shifted her gaze down the cellblock. There were at least a dozen cells in this one, and still more blocks up and down the main passage. Freeing everyone only a handful at a time would take forever. There had to be a faster way, like a control panel or something.

Regina sidled up to her. "I can see what you're thinking,

and you're right. This would be a crap ton easier if there was a main switch to turn off all the shock bars at once."

"Exactly." She shifted her gaze to the cellblock's arched entrance. "The sooner we release everyone, the more of a force we'll be to reckon with."

"Nora and the Norseman took May Belle back the other way to see if those cells are full too." Reg dug a painted fingernail into his wig and scratched. "But they *should've* been back by now."

Yes, they should've. "How about I go see if I can find them, and a control panel of some sort, while you and your boots take over running the show here?"

Reg grinned down at her. "Honey, if there's one thing I know, it's how to run a show."

"If I'd made it to Vegas, I might've found that out." The corners of her mouth twitched up. "My friends and I had tickets to your revue at the Vive Versailles."

"*When* we get back, you and your posse get back-stage passes. Now." Reg pulled her into a bone-squeezing hug. "Get going, girl. I've got this."

"Okay. Just keep an eye out. I don't know where all the aliens suddenly disappeared to, but they can't be far." She stepped back, nodded, then trotted out to the main corridor.

The passageway seemed unending, and there was no sign of anything remotely control-panel-like. Five turns later, a door came into view. An honest-to-god, wide, gleaming white (of course) door with a circular spinning wheel—like a submarine hatch.

Bingo.

That could be their way out, if it was unlocked and didn't lead to the vacuum of space.

A garbled shout came from behind her, and she whipped around to face whatever had made the sound. Two of those damn pasty-faced aliens charged toward her, their wiry, long limbs pumping as they shouted words she couldn't understand, their quick-silver eyes squinted with determination.

"Shit." Time to find out where that door would take her.

FOUR

Misgivings flitted in Sovah's gut as he moved his gaze around the bridge of the grays' vessel. Boarding these barges was usually met with more resistance. So why had his team of sentinels secured the bridge with only a token amount of opposition?

Sentry Commander Guan Waterdiver stepped onto the raised captain's dais and leaned close. "Something feels wrong, Captain."

Even Guan sensed it—though the young male had the intuition of a more seasoned officer, which was why he had been promoted to Sentry Commander at barely twenty-eight sun migrations.

Sovah rubbed his hand over the smooth skin of his chin. "Like this was too easy."

Suspiciously easy, the pirate captain just a feather too cooperative. He wrinkled his nose as a wave of annoyance washed over him.

"Exactly," Guan murmured back, his narrow-eyed gaze on the pirate captain, cuffed and seated to the left of the floor-to-ceiling view screen. "His eyes dart around too much."

Sovah frowned. "How can you tell?"

The grays' eyes had no discernable pupil, just solid monochromatic shading varying in each individual from silver to black. Similar to the genetically enhanced hunting vision many from the raptor clan had retained from their ancestors.

"It is not easy to detect, but there is a faint ripple in the direction they move their eyes."

How had he not known this? He focused on the pirate's pewter eyes. "I see nothing."

At least with a raptor's hunting vision, the pupil was outlined so it was easy to tell which direction a Raptorclaw was looking.

"It is near impossible to see. I had to go through specialized training to learn what to look for."

"All right, watch him and the others closely. In the meantime, I need two of your sentinels to accompany me to the cargo holds to free any Alliance civilians who may have been abducted by this lot."

"Of course, Captain." Guan pointed to two of his crew—both from the Waterdiver clan—standing at attention nearby. "Sentries Colm and Ashma, attend the captain."

The sentinels touched the first two fingers of their right hands to their snowy-white, feathered foreheads in salute. "Yes, Sentry Commander."

Sovah gave Guan a nod of thanks. "I will contact you as soon as we have cleared out enough cells to hold the bridge crew."

A short time later, Sovah strode through the corridor on the cargo level, the two sentinels in his wake. His wings brushed and bumped against the bulkhead of the gleaming white passageway with every step. Clearly, the grays' engineers had not taken into account the larger wingspans of Raptorclaw Bezchians when designing their crafts. Even his smaller-in-stature Waterdiver escorts must have felt a similar constraint. Thank the mercies that he did not suffer from claustrophobia.

On the positive, as far as pirates went, they were obsessively fastidious about their vessels. Even their cargo holds were immaculate, as if they cared about their acquisitions. In any other situation, it would have been considered admirable.

But there was nothing admirable about piracy in any form.

A soft huff escaped through his nose. The real issue that he was trying to distract himself from was the ever-present sense of unease in his belly. It had not lessened upon leaving the grays' bridge. In fact, it seemed to be intensifying, like a looming storm. Not that there was anything he could do about it unless or until that storm broke.

This is probably the last gray vessel I will apprehend.

Or the last vessel ever. Funny how it seemed like a mere half-a-sun migration ago he had accepted command of *Axiom*. Now, he was on his final patrol to the edge of Alliance space. How had time gone by so quickly?

"Turn right at the next intersection ahead, Captain."

He grunted his acknowledgement to Sentry Ashma. A couple more turns, and they should be at the entrance to the cargo hold.

The soft *pat-pat* of hurried footfalls reached his ears, coming from around the corner of the intersection to the passageway they now approached. He stopped just before the turn and raised one hand to the sentinels at his back. Whoever it was, they were coming his way, a distressed gasping to their breathing.

He braced himself, ready to apprehend the being when it emerged. Closer…closer…

A wingless, humanoid figure hurtled around the corner and slammed into his chest. A yelp of surprise escaped it…no, *her*. A female. Fire filled his veins where blood should have been, consuming him with heat as he closed his arms around her smaller stature. The scent of the summer air currents over the ocean surrounded him, and a sigh of contentment seemed to flow not only from his mouth but from every pore of his body.

I have waited all my life for her.

Where in the name of the immortals had this euphoria come from? He gazed down at the wild mess of chin-length silver hair as she tipped her head back and her sky-blue eyes met his.

And he was hers.

A sense of giddy wonder flooded him. This female—wingless though she might be—was meant to stand with him, and he with her. To deny the rightness of her soft curves against him, the glow of life in her pinkened cheeks, the way her full lips parted, would be like denying his own soul.

She squirmed in his embrace, pushing her fists against the uniform fabric of the *omlek* covering his chest, and he released her. By the eternal ones, she was a vision in her loose-fitting, two-piece, silky blue garment, matching cover robe, and bare feet. He lowered his gaze to where her hands clutched two items to her chest. Ah, she had foot coverings, which were as unsuitable for running as bedroom slippers. Which was exactly what they appeared to be.

"Are you unharmed?" He leaned a fraction closer, *not* because he longed to inhale her scent again. He simply wanted to...to....

All right, getting another whiff of her was part of the reason. He inhaled through his nose as subtly as he could. Ah, yes, the delectable scent was all hers.

The corners of her mouth turned down, and she shook her head. "I can't understand you."

Yet he could understand her peculiar dialect of Latii. It was possible her translator implant had been damaged during her captivity. The grays should have fixed it, though. Communication was important, even for a being who was viewed as nothing more than a commodity.

"Captain...."

"I see, Sentry Ashma. We need a working translator for her."

"Not that—"

The heavy thud of more footsteps cut through the haze of bliss surrounding him then two grays charged around the corner. The beautiful female gasped and flattened her back against the bulkhead, a wild desperation in her eyes. That was evidence enough that she was part of their elicit cargo and had somehow escaped.

But the pirates' attention was on him, not the female. A double screech of dismay filled the corridor then the grays turned and ran in the opposite direction. He raised his stunner and fired, but the gutter-scum ducked low, turning left down another passageway.

Well, that was embarrassing. The female would never view him favorably if he could not protect her when necessary. He turned to face her, an apology on his tongue, only to see her curvy backside running back down the passageway from whence she had come.

"Wait!"

She looked over her shoulder then tossed her foot coverings in his direction as if to thwart him from chasing after her. They fell harmlessly to the deck.

Whose side did she think he was on, anyway?

"Captain?" Sentry Colm's rough voice drew his attention back to the here and now.

He was the captain, and the sentinels awaited his command. He blew out a sigh and waved one hand in the general direction the grays had gone. "You two apprehend the grays. I will meet you in the cargo hold's entrance once I have retrieved the female."

"Yes, Captain," they responded in unison then trotted off with their stunners in hand.

He bent to retrieve the discarded slippers, the slippery sky-blue material still warm from being clutched in her hands. They were so tiny, barely the length of one of his hands. He raised his gaze to stare down the now-empty corridor. Her appearance had been as unexpected as it was welcomed. Who was she? And more importantly, how could he convince her to trust him even though she did not understand his words?

Ava huffed along a corridor that looked exactly like every other corridor on the damn ship. White and shiny, without a speck of dust or dirt in sight. Yep, aliens were real, and the ones who'd abducted her sorry ass were a bunch of neatniks.

If only they all looked like the big guy she'd just escaped from…mm-mmm. If the gray ones had dangled *him* in front of her to begin with, she'd have taken one look into those amber eyes and walked herself right into that cell, no questions asked.

It all comes back to marketing, fellas.

How many different aliens were there around here, anyway? She turned her head to cast a quick glance behind her. Nope, no sign of pursuit by anyone, including Mr. Seven-Feet-of-Winged-Yumminess. And, nope, the twinge of disappointment in her chest didn't mean anything.

Just because he was hot, with warm brown skin and the perfect amount of silver in his…hair? It wasn't really hair though, was it? More like feathers. Yeah, two little gray owl-like tuffs on either side of his forehead and a cap of gray and black feathers to match his wings. Oh, and he'd smelled yummy, too. Like a barely-there hint of vanilla.

Ugh, time to stop thinking about him like a potential ally. Sure, he'd fired off a shot at the gray baddies chasing her, but he'd missed. There was a very good chance he was trying to steal her from them. That she was nothing more than a commodity to him.

Could that be what all the bouncing around earlier had been about? Were the winged aliens hi-jacking the gray aliens? If she threw her lot in with the new guy, was there any chance of convincing him to take her and her friends back to Earth?

So many what ifs.

She approached a large circular hatch-like opening in the wall. What a random place for a doorway, one that didn't match any of the other normal, rectangular doorways she'd seen so far. She slowed to a stop and cautiously leaned forward to peek around the edge.

It was some sort of tube, leading to another part of the ship. The circumference of the passage was at least fifteen feet around. And the hallway on the other end was done in blues, creams, and golds, not monotonous white on white. She lowered her gaze to the floor of the tube. A big-ass steaming cow turd sat near the dead center of it. No waste-absorbent flooring here. Had May Belle wandered off and that was why Nora and Axill were taking so long getting back?

Sure hope they're okay.

But why would they have let the cow out of their sight in the first place? Something must have happened, and she might be her friends' only hope of escape now. She swallowed against the knife-edge of panic rising up.

I got this. I do.

If she could run a thriving, international cosmetic company, she could figure out how to free everyone from these aliens. How hard could it be?

Besides, a commitment was a commitment, unspoken or not. And she'd committed to getting her friends out of here. First order of business: get May Belle back to the cellblocks, preferably without getting caught, then figure it out from there.

She cast another glance behind her. Still no one coming. Okay then, time to find out where this tube led. She stepped over the low threshold. The icy bite of the metal floor under her bare feet drew a squeak from her. What had she been thinking, sacrificing her slippers for the sake of efficiency?

No time for regrets. The only direction now was forward. She skirted May Belle's package and approached the tube's exit. Now, why in the world would the hole on this end be so much wider than the hole on the other end?

"Aah!" The sharp exclamation came from behind her, cutting through her focus.

She whipped around to face the danger, and her heart attempted to lodge itself in her throat. Dammit, the sexy winged alien had found her! And he was still as hot as he had been when she'd been plastered against his chest. His huge form filled the opposite opening, the toes and heels of her size ten slippers peeking out of his large hand.

Big hands equals… Oh, now just stop that *line of thinking immediately.*

He extended his other hand and babbled something at her. The words made no more sense than they had before, but the beckoning gesture was clear in any language. *Come here.*

Okay.

She took a step toward him, then another, and another, drawn forward by some invisible force. And his smile. It was as charming as smiles could get.

Whoa, whoa, whoa. Stop, you idiot.

Her body obeyed, even though the magnetic pull still

teased at her. How could she be so ready to fall into his arms without knowing who he was or why he wanted her? This was not normal, not by any stretch of the imagination.

"Yeah, not today, Satan." She forced herself to turn and sprint the rest of the way back, hopping over the threshold.

Warmer air surrounded her. *Run, run, as fast as you can.*

Winged-Guy shouted behind her, then his heavy footfalls clanked against the floor of the tube.

Thump. Thump. Thump. Squelch.

A snarl of words followed the sound of cow shit obeying the laws of physics under the applied pressure of a boot. She pushed down the laugh struggling to escape and forced herself not to look back.

Thank. You. May Belle.

Now, to focus on finding the cow without getting caught.

Sovah watched the wingless female's fetching, round backend receding down the corridor. Again. Mercy to the stratosphere, she had trust issues. At least she was aboard his ship now, and easier to locate via her unregistered biological reading.

He gave his wrist comm a tap. "Deputy Captain Rota, clear all personnel from the docking level corridors, and inform Sentry Commander Guan that I am temporarily disengaging the docking tube." The female had rounded a corner and was out of sight. "We have a runner aboard *Axiom*. Possibly two. One is a humanoid female, the other…" He lowered his gaze to his boot and frowned. "I have no idea, but it made a mess in the docking tube."

"Yes, Captain."

He placed his hand against the tube wall and raised his foot. Brown ooze stuck in the traction ridges of his boot sole, and some had squished up the sides. That was certainly disgusting. How many of his predecessors could brag that they had stepped in feces during their retirement patrol?

Not. A. Single. One.

And *brag* was a poor choice of words.

The soft, warbling purr of approaching cleaning 'bots interrupted his thoughts, and he blew out a sigh. If the 'bots had feelings, they would be perturbed at the mess he was about to track aboard. But they did not, and he had a couple of runners to catch, right after he picked up the required implements.

"Doctor Kirla, I am coming your way for a portable translator and a bio-scanner."

"I will meet you in the corridor, Captain," Kirla Rockdweller replied in her chirpy voice.

He stepped out of the tube into *Axiom*'s passageway as the cleaning 'bots floated in to do their job, then gave the control lever a yank. The docking hatch closed with a *swoosh* followed by the clank of the tube disengaging from the other ship. It would retract fully once the mess was cleaned up, and the 'bots had attached themselves to the vessel's hull to await retrieval.

Moments later, he approached the science and health department. Kirla was waiting in the doorway holding the requested items, the streamlined black feathers of her wings flitting as if she were ready to fly.

"One portable translator and a reader for you, Captain."

"Thank you, Doctor." He accepted the thumb-shaped device and slipped it into the chest pocket of his omlek. Then took the bio-scanner, turning in a slow circle.

Bleep.

Ah, there she was—the biological reading that did not match anyone in the crew registry. Unless it was the creature who had left its mark in the tube. He turned a little farther.

Bleep.

The second reading was for a much larger being who, unlike the humanoid female, moved at a leisurely pace.

"Got them both." But which one should he go after first?

"Do you require assistance with the runners, Captain?"

He lowered the scanner. "If you would not mind tracking down the nonhumanoid."

All indications were that the creature was not agitated and therefore would be less combative. More importantly, Kirla's personality was gentle, which made her the right choice to send after the meandering mystery creature. The female humanoid, on the other wing, was unarmed and frightened, which made her more likely to spread her talons and fight.

"No problem," Kirla replied.

He gave the doctor a quick nod. "Your target is heading toward the hangar bay, which might be a good place to stow it until we figure out a more feasible solution."

"On my way." Her wings fluttered as she turned away. "Good hunting, Captain."

FIVE

Ava trailed her fingertips against the cool smoothness of the wall as she moved forward along the hallway, listening for anything, or anyone. So far, the *anyones* had not made an appearance, except for the couple of times voices had sent her scurrying in a different direction. Now, all she heard was the faint whisper of air circulating through vents.

Given the noticeable variety of color, and that the hallways were at least twice as wide, and tall, it seemed like a safe bet that this ship did not, in fact, belong to the gray guys. That left Sexy Winged Guy and his friends. They must've somehow captured and boarded the ship she'd been on.

Another genius deduction, Sherlock.

So, what did this all mean for her, her friends, and all the other abductees?

The muffled tread of approaching footsteps reached her ears. Someone was coming her way and not trying to hide themselves by tiptoeing around. She cast a frantic glance up and down the empty hallway. Not so much as an alcove in which to hide. She pressed her back against a recessed portion of the wall…because what else could she do?

Swoosh.

The wall behind her disappeared, and she stumbled backward into a room. Whoa. What the hell?

Swoosh.

The door closed, and the subdued lighting brightened. A motion sensor? There must've been one outside too, and that was how the door had been triggered. Interesting. This could buy her a little time to regroup and figure out a better plan to get back to the other ship. Whoever was out there would need to search a lot of rooms before getting to this one.

She turned and breathed out a gasp of awe. A row of windows lining the opposite wall gave her a clear view of the side of a blocky spaceship. She moved forward, skirting the extra-long, black, rectangular table and widely spaced backless stools until she stood a few feet from the window.

No vertigo.

That was a refreshing change from her usual nose-in-a-book, drink-in-hand, aisle-seat-hugger, airline-passenger self. Kinda hard to fall out of a sealed window in space, right? She stepped closer until her nose was centimeters from the glass—or whatever it was the aliens used for windows.

The ship floating outside must belong to the gray aliens who'd kidnapped her stupid ass…and where her friends still were. It was just her against the winged aliens over here. Well, her and May Belle.

A sense of futility pressed down on her, threatening to flatten her into the floor and drown her with black waves of despair. What chance did she have to get out of here, save her friends, *and* get back to Earth? No weapons, no defenses…no goddamn experience with non-human species. Not to mention one massive language barrier. Yet, somehow, she had to figure out a way to do exactly that.

That's me, a one-woman commando.

What she really needed was an entire herd of cows—

Swoosh.

She spun to face the door. Sexy Winged Guy stepped into the room and the door slid shut behind him. Damn, he'd found her fast. So much for having time to plan a great escape. But, wow, those eyes of his. What was it about them that made it impossible to look away, or, for the life of her, kick her brain back into gear?

The alien moved forward, one cautious step at a time, as if trying not to spook her. He was a cat stalking her little mousey self, each movement flowing into the next until he stood facing her across the wide table. Lordy, that was *not* a comforting analogy at all. She swallowed hard against the large knot forming in her chest.

Too close. He was way too close, even with ten feet of table between them. With those wings of his, he could easily fly right over it and pin her to the window or the floor. She allowed her gaze to glide down over his uniform-clad chest…and it *was* a uniform he was wearing. It had to be. The other two white-winged aliens from earlier had been wearing them too, but his had more military-type decorations. A form-fitting, dark blue, sleeveless, all-his-abs-clearly-defined type of uniform. Her breath hitched. Maybe it wouldn't be so bad if he did pin her, somewhere.

A faint whiff of vanilla teased her nose, and burning desire like she'd never experienced before exploded to life between her legs.

What the ever-loving hell?

Sexy Winged Guy leaned forward and she snapped her gaze back to his. That seemed to freeze him in place, as if he were waiting for her next move. Then he held up some sort of thumb-sized, alien techy-looking device and murmured a single word. It was gibberish, the word, but his deep voice rolled over her like distant thunder on a warm afternoon. Comforting because there was distance, yet exciting with the promise of possibility. Which did nothing to ease the yearning restlessness in her girly bits.

All she could do was watch as he set the device down on the table and slid it exactly halfway across. Then he withdrew his hand, stood up straight, and gave her a nod as if everything was fine. Nothing weird about the situation at all.

Was he *giving* her the device? Why? Was it a trap that'd shoot out a beam to immobilize her the moment she touched it? Chrissake, that sounded like something a UFO conspiracy theorist would come up with, not her.

Sexy Winged Guy touched two fingers to his full lips and moved them outward. "Peryk."

This time, the strange word seemed to caress her breasts, and her nipples hardened. Her goddamn sixty-year-old, haven't-been-touched-quite-like-this-*ever* nipples suddenly wanted to play? What the hell was this…this…*magic*?

She folded her arms in front of her boobs as casually as possible then narrowed her eyes at him. "Stop doing that."

The corners of his mouth turned down in a perplexed frown. He couldn't possibly have missed the sharp little nibs poking against the silk of her pajama top, could he?

He pointed at her then tapped his ear, and realization dawned like a sunray from behind a storm cloud.

"It's a *translator*?"

He grinned and nodded. "Tran-lay-er."

Well now, *that* she understood. He wanted to talk to her and was giving her the means to do so through his alien technology. All she had to do was reach out, meet him halfway, and take it. Which meant uncrossing her arms and exposing said nibs again.

I couldn't have brought my baggy fleece PJs on my trip, oh nooo.

She ran her tongue over her lips, and Sexy Winged Guy's amber eyes riveted to the action. Now that was an interesting response, and a way to keep him distracted from her boobs. She hunched forward and extended her arm toward the translator, keeping her gaze on him. If he made any move to grab her, she was ready to jump back.

She closed her hand around the device, drew it toward her then raised it to her chest. "Okay, now what?"

More gibberish came from his mouth.

"I still don't understand."

"Nyouuu willl innn a tiime."

"Oh!" The device *spoke*. "It's *English*."

He said more, and the device spoke again, "It is a portable translator with the capacity for recognizing millions of languages."

Neat! "And those are your words I'm hearing from it?"

"Yes." This time the translation was nearly instantaneous. "Well, I'll be damned."

He lowered his strong, square chin a bit, as a small smile ghosted over his sensual, full lips. "I sincerely hope not."

A laugh bubbled out of her.

His crooked grin widened, and humor lit his eyes. "I understand you because I have a translator implant."

He tapped a finger behind his right ear. A *taloned* finger. He had talons instead of fingernails, which made some sort of rational sense given his other owl-like features.

"Okay, so who *are* you?" And would she have to fight her way out of this room?

Her voice was low and melodious to Sovah's ears, like a joyous morning song. And the way her eyes lit up once she understood how the portable translator worked, that it was a tool to help them communicate, had his heart thudding in his chest.

"I am Sovah Raptorclaw, captain of *Axiom*, a Bezchian vessel of the Galactic Alliance of Planets Protectorship. And you are?"

"Ava Martin." She cleared her throat. "Erm, retired business-woman."

So, a merchant, which likely made her inquisitive, self-assured, and bold. Characteristics he respected in any being.

He extended his hand holding her slippers. "I believe these are yours."

A faint pink color bloomed on her cheeks, and she

reached out to accept the silky foot covers. "Thank you, Captain."

"Please, Merchant Ava Martin, take a perch." He waved one hand in the direction of the stool next to her. "There is much to discuss."

She set her slippers on the tabletop, but the translator she clutched to her breast as though it was a touchstone anchoring her. Not an unusual action for one who had been abducted.

He lowered himself onto the perch to his right then rested his forearms on the table, hands clasped as she hoisted herself onto a matching perch across from him. "I assure you, Merchant Martin, you will be returned to your planet of origin post haste. Grays, as you know, can be aggressive in their quest for living cargo—"

"Excuse me, but no, I *don't* know. Are the grays the aliens who abducted us? Why'd they do that?"

"Well, yes, they are." He pushed the corners of his mouth down into a frown. "That is part of my job as a Protectorship officer, to eliminate their illegal activities. We have done so for many sun migrations. However, their bellwether has eluded us. Until we find it, they will continue to prey on the unsuspecting—"

"What's a bellwether?"

"Their... base vessel, where they report to their leaders—"

"Oh, okay. Like a mothership. I got it. Now, what's a sun migration?"

She definitely had the inquisitive part down. "It is the Bezchian measurement of time for our planet to travel around our sun. Which is three-hundred sixty-two days."

"Ah, you mean a year." She nodded. "And a Bezchian is… what?"

"*I* am a Bezchian." Surely in her field she had met others like him.

"So, a Bezchian is an alien with giant feathery wings."

"No. A Bezchian is a *being* from the planet Bezchi." He leaned back and studied her face. There was no sign of duplicity, so what was her game? "*Alien* is rather insulting, you know."

Her beautiful blue eyes narrowed. "Excuse me again, then, Captain. This is my first abduction, so you're going to have to bear with me."

"The polite term is off-worlder." There was a lot she did not seem to know. A suspicion niggled at the edge of his thoughts. "What planet are you from, Merchant Martin?"

"Ms. It's *Ms.* Martin. And I'm from Earth."

Urth came from her mouth, but his translator said *Soil*. Either way, there were no planets by either name in all of the Alliance. Which could only mean one thing: The grays had expanded their territory to outside Alliance control. He propped his forehead against his palm, and a low groan slipped out.

"What's wrong?"

He met her gaze from under his hand. "It sounds like your planet is being harvested by the grays."

She blinked with steady deliberation once, twice…four times. Then pursed her lips and nodded. "That'd explain a lot. They've been doing it for a long time, I think."

"How long?"

"Generations, maybe? There are stories going back centuries. A century being a hundred…sun migrations."

So long? That was worrisome. The failure of the Protectorship—*his* failure—to stop them was hurting the beings of another planet outside his jurisdiction. *Her* planet. This should not affect him so, but now the situation seemed personal.

Ms. Martin sniffed and wrinkled her long, narrow nose. "You still have cow crap on your boots, don't you?"

"Ah, so, the creature loose aboard my ship is called a *cow*, then?"

"Yeah. Big, docile, milk-producing animal."

Milk was not all the creature produced.

"I see." He lowered his hand back to the table. "Being that your planet is not part of the Galactic Alliance of Planets, I have had no experience with cows. But it sounds similar to the *vava* of Bezchi."

She drew her thin eyebrows together and lowered her gaze to the translator. "I don't get it, then. If no one from the Alliance has ever been to Earth, how does this thing know English?"

"Because you speak an unusual dialect of Latii." Which meant there was a possible connection between the Ing tribe of Nahrung and her planet. She did have striking physical similarities to them.

"Huh. Wouldn't have guessed that."

He would not have guessed that a female from a planet he had never heard of would intrigue him so. "Tell me about your incarceration with the grays. Was it just you and the cow? How did you become separated?"

"No, there were other humans… Earthlings. We dis-covered a way to escape our cells and were trying to help others—not all of them were from Earth either, by the way. Anyway, I went looking for a control to open all the cells when a couple of grays found me, so I ran. Y'know, since it seems like you're here to help us, maybe we can go back and check on my friends?"

Her tentative trust in him was a step forward in their relationship. He gave her a warm smile and rose to his feet. "Of course, Ms. Martin. My sentinels have control of the pirates' ship, so locating your friends should be a simple matter."

He waited for her to don her slippers and come around the table then fell in step with her heading toward the door. She was indeed inquisitive, self-assured, and bold. And small. Barely reached his mid-biceps—

A vibration passed through the soles of his boots, followed by the ear-assaulting screech of the proximity alarms. Every protective instinct unfurled in him. He reached for Ms. Martin, pulling her to his chest as he drew his wings around her and pushed her to the floor. Then her small, and exceedingly soft, body was partly under him. Her breath whooshed out with a soft "oof," fanning over his cheek as they ended up nose-to-nose…and nearly lips-to-lips.

This may be the best action I have taken in my long, solitary life.

The slow blink of her sky-blue eyes seemed to say that she agreed. Blessed ancient ones, if only she would kiss him. As if she had heard his wish, she lifted her head, closing the space between their mouths—

"Captain." Rota's voice cut through the fog invading his brain. *"The grays' bellwether is approaching off our port!"*

The *bellwether*?

He drew back and rolled over partway, pushing away an ache of regret. He locked his gaze onto the scene outside the conference room window. Yes, the grays' cargo vessel was still there, but beyond that was a much larger vessel. So big that only a portion of its monstrous disc-shape was visible through the window.

"Engage the net! Engage the—"

A brilliant flash filled the room, and he squeezed his eyes shut, raising a wing to spare Ms. Martin from the worst of the glare as the bellwether activated its light-drive. When he lowered it to look moments later, only the star-studded blackness of space was visible. They were gone, both vessels, with all the living "cargo" and a third of his crew.

Shit

SIX

Ava bounced along like she was frog-walking just to keep up with the captain as he hauled her through the corridor by her hand.

I almost *kissed him.*

Would've kissed him, if not for the interruption. After which, he'd had the nerve to try to leave her in the conference room. Tried to pass her off to some unknown crew member to take her to a "safe place." As if there was a safe place inside a giant floating space can.

Now there was an analogy he probably wouldn't appreciate, if he even knew what a can was. At least it hadn't taken him long to realize that she was having none of his dump-and-run plan. Those were *her* friends who'd just been re-abducted, and she'd be damned if anyone was going to exclude her from rescuing them. Hence the reason she was biting back her true feelings about the way he was hauling her along behind him like an errant child.

They rounded a corner, and he came to an abrupt stop, pulling her hard against his side. "Watch out."

"What?" She followed his gaze downward to another cow patty. Two square floating Romba-like machines seemed to be consuming it. "Oh."

Ew.

"How much does this cow of yours defecate?"

"You'd be surprised."

"I *am* surprised." He released her hand and tapped a slim, band-like device attached to his wrist. "Doctor Kirla, have you secured the second runner?"

"*Yes, Captain,*" a musical female voice responded. "*She appears to be a non-aggressive, agricultural animal. I have secured her in the hangar bay for now while I work on creating a suitable synthetic grain.*"

"Good work. Thank you." He tapped his wristband again then extended his hand toward her. "We must hurry."

Yes, they did, lives were at stake. She slipped her hand back into his. "Lead on."

Two turns and an elevator ride upward later, she trotted through an open doorway into a wide, semi-circular room. The navy, gold, and cream color scheme continued here, and it looked very much the way a spaceship bridge should look, according to Hollywood. Panels of blinking lights, a wrap-around window with a view of the stars, and in the center of it all, one of those cushioned stool things he'd called a perch. Unlike the ones in the conference room, though, this had a narrow gold vertical back-bar as wide as her hand. The bar was topped with a cushioned headrest, which matched the seat.

Aliens—no, *Bezchians*, because everyone on the bridge sported feathered wings of some sort—stood at stations.

"Report, Deputy Captain." Captain Sovah released her hand and moved to sit on the weird stool-perch then settled his huge wings to either side of the bar and under the headrest.

So, the bar provided back support for the Bezchians. Kind of a smart design for their physical build, really.

"Sentry Commander Guan has activated his tracer." A tall, winged woman turned to face the captain.

She was stunning, in a wild, Valkyrie-warrior sort of way that not even her military-esque uniform could quite tame. Younger than the captain by at least fifteen years. The cap of short feathers on her head were black and gold, and flowed straight back, giving her the appearance she was perpetually facing a strong wind.

Captain Sovah nodded. "We should be able to follow them, as long as they are not too far from us. Engage pur—"

"Captain." Another Bezchian looked up from her station, a short, black plume bobbing over her forehead. Of all things, this one resembled a quail. "Protectorship Command is responding to our intent-of-pursuit alert. Chief Commissioner Strauss Landwalker requests dialogue with you."

"Put him on the center viewer, Warden Tiya."

Tiya returned her attention to her station, and punched a green button with a stubby, taloned finger. A section of the star field in the window flickered, and a ruddy-red-complected Bezchian appeared. This guy looked older than the captain, and sported fluffy, faded gray wings that would've made an ostrich envious.

Curiouser, and curiouser.

"We received your intent-of-pursuit, Captain Raptor-claw." The guy's voice had the quality of gravel under a car tire. "Request denied."

A soft gasp of surprise went through the bridge, and every feathered head swiveled to look at the Chief Commissioner.

Captain Sovah leaned forward. "Chief, several of my crew are aboard the grays' cargo vessel, including my sentry commander, who has activated his tracer. We can apprehend them swift—"

"I understand, Captain. We have ordered *Maxim*'s captain to track down the grays' bellwether. You are to complete the return portion of your final patrol."

The captain's jaw clenched visibly. "*Maxim* is two days away, even at top speed."

"You will give them the tracer's frequency and let them handle it." The chief glared pointedly at the captain. "Command wants you back *unharmed*, Sovah. *Maxim* is already underway. They will retrieve your crew."

"My crew is my responsibility, Strauss."

"And *you* are *ours*."

Okay, that was harsh, especially when everything the captain said made sense. The grays did have his people, after all. And one thing she'd learned in the earliest days of growing her business; a good boss *always* took care of their own.

Besides, the way the crew was looking from him to the Chief Commissioner and back, it seemed like they weren't happy with the order either. Maybe a little advocacy wouldn't hurt.

She took a step forward. "Excuse me." The Chief Commissioner jerked his gaze to hers. "There are a lot of people like me being held prisoner on that ship, too. If what Captain Sovah told me is true, they're going to be sold into slavery, along with his crew. There's really no time to waste here."

"Raptorclaw." The chief's attention flicked back to the captain. "You will follow Command's order and be back in port on schedule. Am I clear?"

"Yes, Chief." The response was forced through the captain's clenched teeth.

Strauss the Louse waved his hand in her direction. "And remove this civilian from your bridge. Her presence there is against regulations. We will question her once you arrive at Protectorship Command."

"But—"

"That is an *order*, Captain."

The screen snapped back to the starfield, and a heavy silence settled over the bridge. Everyone's attention was fully on their leader now.

The captain stared straight ahead, his jaw working for a moment. "Continue on patrol course, Warden."

Tiya opened and closed her mouth then turned back to her station. "Yes, Captain."

He was actually *not* going after the grays? This was unbelievable, unacceptable.

Ava propped her fists on her hips. "You're just going to leave them all to a fate worse than death then?"

"What would you have me do, Ms. Martin? Disobey a direct order?"

"*Yes*." Because that was what a leader did.

His narrow-eyed scowl landed on her, hot enough to vaporize her on the spot. "The crew of *Maxim* are in charge of the mission now. Deputy Captain, escort Ms. Martin to Doctor Rockdweller for a temporary translator then find her suitable quarters."

Wait, what? He was *dismissing* her? Just like that?

"Yes, Captain." The Valkyrie fixed her with an icy expression and all the angry words withered like prey in an eagle's talons. Geez, these people had mastered *the look*. "Follow me please, Ms. Martin."

As if she had a choice. Besides, keeping company with the captain had lost its luster. She gave him a glare of her own as she turned away.

We'll be having words later, mister.

In the elevator, the Valkyrie turned her sharp black-eyed gaze on her. "I am Deputy Captain Rota Raptorclaw, but please call me Rota."

Raptorclaw? Was she somehow related to Captain Raptorclaw? Cousin, sister…wife? Her gut twisted. Not that there was any reason for regret at this point. She had met the guy all of twenty minutes ago, give or take.

And, my bad for assuming he had a backbone.

"I'm Ava Martin from Earth." She curled her fingers tighter around the translator and gave her free hand a dismissive wave. "Which apparently no one around here has ever heard of before."

Rota tilted her head to one side. "Your planet is not a member of the Galactic Alliance, which explains why you do not have a translator implant."

"So I've heard." She raised the portable device to chest level. "But this one's been working fine."

"Hmm." Rota's expression softened, a bit. "We will give you a better one. The health and science station is located one level down."

"I don't want anything permanent."

The corners of Rota's mouth twitched upward. "It simply attaches behind your ear and can be put on and off at your convenience. Although, you cannot take it with you when you return to your planet."

"*If* I return." Captain Dumbass hadn't bothered to mention that she wasn't an Alliance citizen to Chief Peckerhead.

Rota shrugged as the elevator door swooshed open. "You will, once Command discovers your planet of origin."

One could only hope. So far, this trip into the cosmos seemed determined to remain an involuntary one on her part.

Sovah held his mouth firm, lips pressed together, and directed his gaze toward the viewer which had hosted Strauss's image moments ago. Storm winds take the chief commissioner for denying him the right of pursuit. Ava was correct in her assessment of the situation, but his wings were as good as clipped.

Words of conciliation had stuck in his throat as her slippered footsteps had moved away from him. Words he did not dare to utter to her. And then the whisper of the lift's doors closing took away that choice as well.

Wait. Come back. I have changed my mind.

But he had not, really. To change his mind would be to defy the rules that governed the safety of the Alliance of Planets and the citizens therein. Disregard for rules allowed chaos and pain to slip in, take over. Destroy lives.

Like Rena's.

The age-old ache of loss settled over him as if a lifetime of sun migrations had not passed since that terrible day. A day his young fledgling-self learned a hard truth that would define his life and set him on the path to his career.

Wind rushed across the plain, roaring in its victory over the long, topaz-color field-grass bowing under its power. It buffeted against his body, tugging at his untried wings with icy claws.

He crouched, tucking his wings close to his back so a sudden updraft would not lift him into the sky. "Please, Rena, I want to go home."

Home where they would be protected from the boiling, angry black clouds overhead. Where the jagged flashes of lightning would not harm them, and they would be safe in Momma's lap from the soul-shaking booms of thunder.

"I am not ignoring a dare, Sovah."

"But, why not?"

Her nose scrunched as she looked down at him for being such a coward. Why could she not see that nothing about the oncoming storm was safe?

"Please, Ree. Momma says to never fly in a storm. You could get hurt." Or killed.

Only full-grown Bezchians were strong enough to

navigate the wind shears, and even then, it was not a thing to take on lightly.

"It is just a little storm, brother mine—"

The sweet scent of warm summer air currents tickled inside his nose, jerking him back to reality before he got lost in the childhood memory. Ava's scent. Too bad the heat in his veins did not dissipate with her absence. If anything, it burned hotter, as if only she could quell it. So had it been since the moment she had slammed into him aboard the grays' vessel.

What was wrong with him, anyway? He was a Protectorship captain, under orders. New orders, now…given to him by his superior. That was what a chain of command was for, to keep everything in order and everyone safe. And in the end, that was what mattered most. Safety.

Guan is not safe. Neither are his sentinels…or Ava's friends, for that matter.

He pushed those thoughts to the darkest recesses of his mind lest they tempt him then allowed his gaze to drift around the bridge. Was it his imagination, or were his normally gregarious officers unnaturally subdued? Every last one of them had their heads lowered as though thoroughly absorbed by whatever was on their control-station consoles.

Warden Tiya lifted her gaze in a covert manner to peek at him and froze. The black feather plume on her forehead bobbed, but otherwise she did not move under his scrutiny.

He gave her a deep frown. "Is there a problem, Warden?"

She opened her mouth, drawing in a breath before

snapping it shut and returning her gaze to her station. "No, Captain."

A stab of disappointment poked at his consciousness. Never in the five sun migrations since she had been assigned to *Axiom* had she ever lied to him. But what could he do about it, call her out when it was very likely she had done it because he had let her down?

This was not how his retirement cruise was supposed to go. Losing even a single member of his crew was unacceptable, and he had lost almost his entire team of sentinels. Yet what recourse did he have?

I could go against Command's orders.

Even Ava—*Ms. Martin*—had figured that out. But if he fell from grace, Command, and possibly even the Alliance, would bring down the rest of his crew as an example. He could not risk their careers in that manner. *Maxim*'s captain was capable and experienced.

He released the mounting resignation with a sigh. "Warden, send Security Commander Guan's tracer code to *Maxim*."

SEVEN

———————✦———————

The trek down a level to the health and science station had been more of the same blue and gold décor. But everything about the station, from the antiseptic-clean scent to the white-uniform-wearing staff, had all but shouted medical clinic. And then, there'd been the unflappable Doctor Rockdweller, the apparent head of the department, who'd clearly never met an Earthling before and had been thrilled to have exclusive access to one in her domain.

Within seconds of Ava's arrival, the slim, swallow-winged woman had installed a kidney-bean-sized translator in the crease behind her ear, chattering about how delightfully adorable May Belle was, and how the ship's food simulator had been programed with a synthetic grain conducive to the cow's biological needs, as well as reduce the amount of waste output. All of which should make Captain Dingleberry deliriously happy.

If Rota hadn't pulled rank on the good doctor, they would've still been there instead of strolling through the three open, heavy-duty blast doors guarding the hangar bay.

Rota didn't break her stride as they entered the pale-gray-toned space beyond. "The doors will open for anyone aboard *Axiom* when not on tactical alert."

"How about when you are on alert?" She let her gaze take in the area. It was ginormous—maybe eight or more football fields in length and width.

"In those instances, only registered crew with the proper codes can access it." Rota pointed with two fingers. "Look there."

She followed the direction indicated, her gaze stopping at the wide, gaping opening filled with black, star-studded space. Nothing between her and the vacuum of nothingness except distance. The all-to-familiar queasy sense of vertigo washed through her, and she pulled in a ragged breath. Was the floor undulating?

Rota closed her hand around her left biceps and drew her to a stop. "Do not worry, Ava. The forcefield is intact and can only be penetrated by ships with clearance to land or depart. Unprotected biological lifeforms cannot float out."

"O-okay." Weird that standing by the conference room window hadn't bothered her, but the openness of the access to the hangar bay had her brain screaming to run back to the safety of the ship's interior hallways.

"Would you like to go stand on the edge at look out? The view is inspiring."

"*No.*" She gave Rota an 'are you out of your mind' stare. "No, um, but thank you."

Safe or not, why tempt fate? Especially with her recent run of luck.

"Mooo." May Belle's lowing drew her gaze to the far side

of the hangar bay, where two Bezchian mechanics were scratching the cow's forehead and murmuring sweetly at her.

A chuckle bubbled up. "Looks like someone has a fan club already."

"A *fan club*?" Rota tilted her head to one side, clearly not understanding the term.

"Admirers."

"Ah, yes. Shall we join them?"

After a few minutes of loving on the displaced bovine, Rota led the way from the bay to the parking hangar running along the starboard side of the ship. The ding-ding of May Belle's cow bell trailed after them, oddly muted in the vastness of the flight deck. Fan club or not, it seemed the cow didn't want to be left behind by the only other Earthling aboard.

At least two dozen smaller ships were parked...or docked, was probably the technical term...along the walls, leaving a wide walkway down the center between them. They were beautiful in the aerodynamic way of military fighters.

"And this." Rota waved in the direction of a sleek, matt-black ship about the length of a 747, only wider and with wedge-shaped wings near the tail end. "This is a Night Stealth, the newest and fastest pursuit ship in the fleet. There are only three of these in existence right now, and Captain Raptorclaw made sure we got one before he retired."

"He's retiring soon?"

"Upon our return to Bezchi, yes."

"Is he always like this? Hard-headed and closed off to other options?" The none-too-subtle bump of May Belle's nose nudged her in the shoulder, and she smoothed her hand over the coarse swirls of hair between the cow's eyes.

Rota's throaty chuckle was tinged with friendly amusement. "He has always been fair and open to the ideas of others, within the confines of our laws. He would not have made captain otherwise. Yet, not even he disobeys a direct order."

A huff escaped. "I guess not."

And she hadn't made the situation any better by arguing with him in front of his crew.

"Come." Rota made a beckoning gesture with one hand then started up the ramp into the Night Stealth.

Guess we're going in.

Which seemed weird for a ship with *stealth* in its name. Maybe it wasn't as top secret as it sounded.

"Gotta go, May Belle." She gave the cow a final pat. "Behave yourself."

She jogged to catch up as Rota disappeared through the open doorway at the top of the ramp.

The inside of the ship was sleeker than the outside, shiny black where the outside had been dull. If there was a polar opposite of the inside of the grays' ship, this was it. Color-wise at least. The Night Stealth could give them a run for their money in cleanliness. And it was silent in an eerie sort of way, as if all sound had been deadened.

"You have probably guessed that the outside is designed to blend in with the darkness of space." Rota had completely donned the mantle of a tour guide. "It also has a stealth cloak as advanced as *Axiom*'s. It even has sleeping quarters in the back for extended missions."

"And this?" Ava waved one hand at the glassed-in enclosure to her right.

"A detainment room."

The dang room was big enough to fit at least seven May Belles—or Captain Raptorclaws. The image of the inflexible, order-obeying captain trapped inside and at her mercy sent a shiver of pleasure trilling down her spine.

She gave her head a small shake to dislodge that inappropriate thought. "Um, so, is that one of those waste-absorbing floors in there?"

Oh, aren't you the master of smooth transitions? Not.

"Yes. A necessary precaution. Some detainees are not always...in peak flight when they are taken into custody." Rota turned away and continued along the straight hallway. "Up here is the cockpit."

Ava hurried to catch up and peered around Rota's wings. The cockpit was pretty average-looking, with two of those headrests-on-a-stick perches, a darkened control panel, and black view screen.

Rota tapped a button, and the panel lit up. "It is about as minimal as it can be, for all the features it has."

"Like what?"

"Sorry, Ms. Martin, that is classified information." Rota met her gaze with an apologetic smile. "And it is not why I brought you in here."

A knot of mild apprehension tightened in her chest. "It's not?"

"There are some things you should know about Captain Raptorclaw. Things that I will only share with you in the anonymity this craft provides."

Oh, geez. This was the big *he's married* reveal, wasn't it? "Like?"

"Like, as noble as I believe your reasons were for fluffing your feathers at Chief Commissioner Strauss in your clan's defense, Sovah is not one to ever defy orders." She huffed a small laugh. "Of course, we have never been in a situation quite like this either...."

There was something in Rota's tone that suggested subterfuge. "So, what? You think he might go after the grays?"

"Possibly. If he was properly...*motivated*." Rota's expectant black gaze captured hers.

I think I like where this is going. "Meaning?"

"Meaning that the only reason Command ordered him back is because they have plans to use him and his exemplary record as a recruiting tool." Rota's lips twisted in annoyance. "There is nothing wrong with this, as such. But I know Sovah well enough to know that his happiness in that role will be fleeting. He has made so many personal sacrifices for them, willingly. What his soul craves now is peace. A life that is steady and uncomplicated. He deserves that, and we all see it. Unfortunately, the stubborn old bird does not know how to prioritize anything above the Protectorship. Not yet, anyway."

And that must be where the motivation part came in. "I bet his wife would have something to say about that."

Ooh, she was so fishing.

Confusion lines appeared across Rota's feathery brow then cleared, and she barked a sharp laugh. "Sadly, a mate is one of the things he sacrificed for his career."

"You mean, you two aren't…?"

"Oh, sweet blue heavens, no! The phoenixes of the Firewing clan matched me happily with my mate many sun migrations ago. And in the raptor clan, we mate for life. Unless tragedy befalls our mate, there is only one. Even then, some do not take another."

"Sorry for assuming." So, if there was no wife, or mate, to motivate him, Rota must believe she could. "Let me be blunt, here. I am not having sex with him to get him to change his mind."

But I wouldn't mind *having sex with him.*

The deputy captain's eyes widened with shock. "I would not suggest it!"

"Good." Damn. "Glad we got that straight."

Rota's laughter filled the space, and she wiped her knuckle under one eye. "Ms. Martin, you are a delight. I do believe showing you this *stealth vessel*, and allowing you time to consider the *possibilities it offers*, will be enough for now."

Oh, so it was like that, huh? Give the Earthling information-ammo then let her decide what to shoot at?

"Okay, so I think I get what you're hinting at, but when laws are broken, *someone* has to go to jail."

"*If* that someone is an Alliance citizen, yes." Rota lowered her chin and gave her an expectant look. "Which you are not."

"I see." This might be what the business world referred to as *an opportunity.*

"Good." Rota's expression softened, the officer melting away into…a friend? "I am glad we have this understanding between us and will leave you to the details. But, now," her vibe returned to dutiful officer mode, and she motioned back toward the door with one hand, "I should get you to your quarters and report back to the bridge. I have been absent long enough."

Rota hustled her off the ship and out of the hangar bay without giving her a chance to say good-bye to May Belle. Although, the cow seemed more interested in chewing her cud while waiting for her fan club to notice her again, anyway.

EIGHT

Sovah leaned forward on his desk perch. The pressure of his fingertips pinching the bridge of his nose brought no relief to the tight band of stress squeezing his head. Plus, it did not seem to matter how far under his desk he stuck his foot, there was no escaping the wafting odor of the cow's fecal matter. Yet another reminder of how quickly everything had turned to shit.

Was there no reasonable way out of this dismal vortex he had been forced into?

Ping.

He opened his eyes a slit and gave the ready room door a hard glare. Whoever was waiting on the other side best not ask him for a favor.

Be fair. It could be someone with an answer to my predicament.

Besides, it was time to get back to his duty, whether he was ready or not. He breathed out a sigh, released his nose from his futile attempt at relief, then gave the door control button a resigned finger tap.

Swoosh.

Rota strode into the ready room, stopped halfway to his desk, then folded her arms in front of her and scowled at him until the doors closed again.

He suppressed a groan. Something pecked at her, and she was about to unload on him. "What do you want, Deputy Captain?"

"For you to do what you know you should."

"You know I cannot." And she knew *why* not.

"Cannot? Or *will* not?" She settled on the perch on the opposite side of his desk. "You live by the rules in the strictest sense, Captain, and now you are trapped by them."

It was the truth, as much as he wished to deny it. "There are consequences to breaking rules."

There always were. His sister had been a statistic of this fact.

"Of course there are, but I challenge you to find one Bezchian aboard this vessel who will not support you."

He set his jaw and narrowed his eyes at her. "Such action could be viewed as treason against the Alliance—"

"Mm." Rota bobbled her head from one side to the other. "Perspective."

He slapped his hand down against the surface of his desk, the sting of the impact burning his palm. "I *cannot* ask that of them, or of *you*."

"Pfft." She waved her hand in a dismissive gesture. "Maybe not the crew, but me...? Honestly, Sovah. How long have you known me?"

That was also true. Rota had always found ways to stretch the letter of the law when necessary and had never received more than a disciplinary wing slap. It was a wonder how he had chosen her to be his successor, her command style was so different.

On the other wing, it was not overly surprising. He had understood and accepted the advantages of having such a different view-point to rely upon, especially in a crisis. And their current situation was easily classified as a crisis.

Rota leaned forward, her black-eyed gaze level with his. "The decision is yours, but you know that I will have your wing, no matter what. In the meantime, Ms. Martin is probably furiously pacing her quarters. I tried explaining to her, but I am not the one who made the decision to follow Strauss's order so literally. She needs to hear from you."

"Cultural differences." He muttered the words as if they somehow explained everything.

What kind of place was her Earth, where challenging a law enforcement captain in front of his officers was acceptable? Perhaps that was the way things were done there, but not here.

"Go talk to her, Sovah."

"And say what, exactly?" He barked a laugh. "Sorry that I am leaving your friends to—as she so aptly put it—*a fate worse than death*?"

Rota stared at him, silent and still as a predator hunting its prey. Which was not a farfetched analogy. She was descended from the elite Kyrja line of seraphic raptors, so she might be very much ready to shred him to pieces. That alone was proof that he had made the right choice for his replacement. Not that he needed proof.

"Fine." He waved his still-tingling hand in her direction. "I will speak to Ms. Martin. Dismissed, Deputy Captain."

"Yes, Captain." She rose from the perch smoothly and moved toward the door then stopped in the open doorway and half-turned. "By the way, I was in such a hurry to return to my bridge duties that I may have…*overlooked* showing Ms. Martin some basic operations of her quarters. Like how to operate the door."

He opened his mouth, the words, *you trapped her in her quarters?* ready to blurt out. But she turned away and the door swooshed closed behind her.

'Overlooked,' my pinfeathers.

Although, she had likely kept Ms. Martin from sneaking away and going after the grays' vessel alone. Always gliding along that fine line, his deputy captain.

He released a small sigh and allowed his wings to droop. A smooth, worry-free final mission was not to be, nor what he wished for. Although, there was no denying that life *would* have been much easier if *Axiom* had never crossed flight-paths with those pirates.

A spasm twisted through his gut. Yet, if they had not, he would never have met *her*. There was only one choice, and that was to face this challenge as he had faced all others: with his wings spread and head high. And his first duty was to pay a visit to Ms. Martin.

He pushed off his perch and inhaled a deep, confident breath through his nose. The acrid smell of cow dung went straight to his brain, and a cough escaped him.

"Merciful immortals." First duty: change boots. *Then* deal with the enchantingly exasperating Earthling.

A very efficient five minutes later, he strode along the

corridor toward Ms. Martin's quarters. Each footfall of his gleaming, *clean* black boots was muffled against the deck.

This is insane.

He still had not a wind's-breath of an idea what to say to her. However, Rota was seldom wrong about anything, so maybe the necessary words would simply come to him. Words that would appease both himself and Ms. Martin. And for some inexplicable reason, her opinion was important to him.

Why? For the potential taste of her sweet lips?

That would be unconscionable. She was not an Alliance citizen and would eventually be returned to her own planet. Still, neither of them were fledglings, so maybe....

No. No good could come from that line of thought.

He came to a stop in front of her doors and pressed his thumb against the chime button. Rota must have chosen this nest for its proximity to the hangar bay. Ms. Martin would want to be close to the cow, the only other citizen of her planet aboard. That would be his choice if he were in her predicament.

His thoughts drifted to the mysterious creature that he had yet to see himself. Good to know it was safely ensconced, and unlikely to deposit more piles of its feces in *Axiom*'s corridors anytime soon.

Why had Ms. Martin not responded yet? He rapped his knuckle against one door. "Ms. Martin?"

A muffled voice came from within.

He leaned closer and pressed one ear near the line where the doors met. "Please repeat yourself."

"How do I open the door?" It sounded as though she had her mouth at the seam.

The corners of his lips twitched, but he dampened the urge to smile. So, Rota's plan had worked. "Computer, executive override for nest two-dash-one-zero-one-two."

The doors slid open with a sigh, revealing Ms. Martin clutching at the belt of a draping dark blue pull-over cover that puddled around her feet. The garment hung on her small frame, covering all the parts he appreciated about her, yet leaving her pale-skinned neck, shoulders, arms...and a hint of cleavage, exposed.

I appreciate those parts too.

Her soft scent was more noticeable now, wafting around him along with the familiar fragrance of the institutional soap used aboard Protectorship vessels.

Her lips parted, and she blinked up at him. "How'd you do that?"

He grinned down at her. "A simple override."

Great Aerie help him, but his fingers itched to slide the cover down her arms to reveal what was hidden underneath.

"You can *do* that?" She tangled the fingers of her free hand through the ends of her damp hair. "What about people's privacy?"

"I have only had to use the privilege once in my entire career. Today." He tilted his head to one side. "May I enter?"

"Oh, right. Sorry." She gathered the cover in her hands and stepped back farther into the room. "Come on in."

"I will have a word with Deputy Captain Raptorclaw for not showing you how to work the door mechanism." A word of thanks, and the admission that she had been correct.

"Well, she was in a hurry." There was a tone of casual dismissal in Ms. Martin's words.

"Not an excuse." He stepped into the room and pointed to the button panel set into the wall to the left of the doors. "This one opens…and this one closes." He gave the latter a tap, and the doors swooshed closed. "Here is the thermostat control, and this one is an emergency call."

She breathed out a sigh. "Stupid that I didn't think to check it out myself. But I did learn that what you call a preen is the same as a bathroom. And I figured out how everything in there works."

"Good." Her eyes were clear now, no sign of the brewing storm that had been there earlier when she had left the bridge.

Those beautiful eyes tracked down his body as far as his hips then back up. "How do you stay in such great shape? I've tried, but…." She glanced down at herself this time.

He clamped down on the spike of desire. "If you are saying that there is something wrong with your body, I can assure you there is not."

The memory of her body half under his in the conference room surfaced. Yes, she was perfectly soft and round in all the right places.

"Well, I'd like to be as svelte as you, but…. How old are you, anyway?"

"Fifty-eight sun migrations."

"I figured we had to be close to the same age." She patted the gentle curve of her belly.

Why did she compare herself to him? "I think you are fortunate not to have to worry about being grounded if you are not 'in shape,' as you say."

She pursed her lips and nodded. "Good point. Well, I'm guessing you didn't stop by to discuss calisthenics with me. Come on in and sit down."

Finally. Although he still had no idea what to say to her, but he had until they were seated and comfortable to come up with something.

She moved ahead of him, the cover flowing over her curves like water. "I have a bone to pick with your garment desoiler, Captain. It destroyed my silk pajamas."

"You mean the blue garment you had on?" He would ask her about the *bone pick* later. It sounded like more than he wanted to deal with right now.

"Yes."

"My apologies, Ms. Martin. Replicator, generate a garment to the specifications of the last one done in two-dash-one-zero-one-two's desoiler."

"Generating," the monotone response came.

"Huh." Ms. Martin huffed. "Another thing I wish I'd known."

A soft chuckle rolled out of him. "Things here must be very different from your home world."

"Yeah." She peered back at him over one shoulder. "Just a little."

All his attention fixated on her face. The shimmer in her blue eyes, the way her pink lips parted just enough to see the even edge of her white teeth.

She stumbled and let out a surprised squeak as she pitched forward. His reflexes went into automatic response mode, and he reached for her, closing his hands around her waist and hauling her back against his chest before she came anywhere near hitting the deck.

By the immortals, the body-warmth of this tiny, wingless female pressed against him was enough to send all his blood rushing to the strategic point where her bottom met his shaft. How could she—an off-worlder he had known for mere hours—affect him so?

"Be careful." He murmured the words next to her ear.

She turned her head partway then ran her little pink tongue over her lips. "I don't think I want to be."

Neither did he, really.

"Captain," she whispered.

"What?" He could not help but whisper back.

"I'm, uh, *hanging out*, so to speak."

Hanging out? Was this some kind of Earth terminology?

She cleared her throat. "The robe shifted, and it's sleeveless. If you let me go, I can fix it."

Oh. He swallowed as a sense of awkwardness descended and released her with care. "Of course."

She adjusted the oversized cover then turned to face him; all the *hanging-out parts* once again hidden under the fabric. "Well. That was…stimulating."

Stimulating was a good word choice. It might take more than a few moments to *un*-stimulate himself. "Are you hurt?"

Redirection of the conversation was a good start.

"I'm fine. Tripped over the hem. I'm kinda a klutz like that sometimes." Her gaze flicked down to his waist, and a furrow appeared between her brows.

"I do not understand *klutz*."

"Clumsy." She raised her gaze again to meet his then

moved closer to trail her fingers down his right hip. "You didn't hurt yourself catching me, did you?"

"No harm done." Not in the way she must mean, at least. "I thank you for your concern."

A flash of guilt crossed her face, and it was impossible not to reach up and trace his own fingers over the softness of her cheek in reassurance—

"Garment generated." The flat, computerized words from the replicator cut through the moment.

Her hand slipped away, and she took a step back. Disappointing, but it was best to keep their relationship professional.

He lowered his own hand and cleared his throat. "I will retrieve your...*pajamas*."

He moved to go around her.

"Ah-ah, Captain." She raised her arm, and his gaze was drawn to the device in her hand.

No, not a device...a stunner. How in a thousand lightning strikes had she gotten ahold of one of— *Shit*. He jerked his hand down to the holster at his hip. Empty. That was *his* stunner. He tamped down the heat of anger rising in his chest. How could he have been so careless?

"You cannot take *Axiom* hostage, you understand?" It was not possible with all the safeguards in place.

"Actually, I was thinking just you and I might take a ride in that lovely little Night Stealth in the hangar bay."

She knew about the Night Stealth? An uneasy thought floated into his mind. Had Rota shown it to her? "Why would we do that?"

"Because someone's got to take charge of this operation,

Captain. And you've made it pretty damn clear that you won't." She wiggled the stunner a bit. "Now, put your hands in the air and turn around."

Hands in the...? Air. Yes, of course. She wanted him to raise his hands high. And at the moment, his cooperation was necessary, so he did as she bade and presented his back to her.

"What are you doing, Ms. Martin?"

"Changing into something that fits...*don't turn around.*"

The urge to look back at her was almost automatic, but he stopped himself at her sharply spoken warning. He would have to be content listening to her shuffling, and the rustle of soft fabric gliding over her skin behind him as he contemplated this unexpected situation.

It was a tantalizing concept, what she proposed. Her forcing him at stunner point to pursue the grays' bellwether and rescue her friends, his crew. Not just tantalizing, but intriguing... Wait, was he seriously considering doing this? Risking every principle he had ever held dear to follow through on a potentially dangerous—some, like himself, would say treasonous—scheme?

Yes. Yes, I am.

"Okay," Ms. Martin announced. "Turn back around, nice and slow."

He did, keeping his hands high and visible. "You know that you could be arrested for this?"

That was not exactly true. As a citizen of a non-Alliance planet, she could return to her own planet so long as he did not press charges. Which, he would not. But she did not need to know that, yet. Let her believe she had the upper wind current. For now.

She jutted her chin out. "I am so beyond caring."

"I see." She really did handle the stunner in a manner indicating she was familiar with similar weapons. Not even a slight tremor in her supposedly untrained hands.

"Out the door and to the right, Captain. I know exactly how to get to the hangar bay, so no tricks. And FYI, I grew up on a farm, and your stunner isn't that different from the guns I learned to shoot."

So, he was right. And completely unsurprised by her revelation. He moved toward the doors, adding *FYI* to his mental list of vocabulary questions to ask her about later.

NINE

God Almighty, she'd lost her ever-lovin' mind. Sunk to a new, all-time low. But how else could she get a seven-foot winged alien…erm, off-worlder…to go along with her crazy plan? By asking him pretty please, with whipped cream and a cherry on top? That would never work.

Besides, it was his own second-in-command who'd planted this crazy idea in her brain in the first place—before locking her inside this cabin. Which had turned out to be a good thing. Gave her plenty of time to come up with a workable plot. Or at least one that sounded good in her head.

The captain pressed the door's open button with one long, taloned finger. The doors parted, swooshing softly, and her gaze was drawn to his fine ass peeking between his folded wings as he stepped into the corridor. Were Bezchian uniforms designed to show off the defined muscular structure of the wearer or what?

Her hostage—because despite his compliance, he wasn't exactly her partner in crime—made as though he was going right toward the hangar, then darted to the left. Dammit. So much for compliance.

She rushed through the doorway, aimed the stunner, then pressed the large round button dead-center of its handle. A pale beam of bluish light shot out of the other end, catching the base of the captain's left wing. He staggered as the wing went limp, the dead weight dragging him to his knees then his hands. How surprisingly Hollywood.

His deferential chuckle filled the ensuing silence. "So, you *do* know how to use that thing."

"Been shooting guns since I was eight."

"Good to know." He braced his hand against the wall and twisted far enough to peer at her over his sagging wing. "You—"

"Talk later. Go now."

"All right." He clambered to his feet, and she stepped back into the open doorway as he made his way past her, using the wall for balance as his wing dragged behind him.

I do not feel guilty. I do not feel guilty.

Oh hell, who was she kidding? She forced her gaze to the back of his feathered head, which helped a little but didn't shut out the accusing shush of feathers trailing along the floor.

A few turns later, they'd passed through the hangar bay doorways, crossed the flight deck, and finally approached the Night Stealth, which was still wide open, thank goodness. All without drawing anyone's attention, mostly because the two mechanics had their heads stuck inside the undercarriage of another shuttle-like craft.

This just might work.

As long as she didn't get ahead of herself or let her guard down. And as long as Captain Raptorclaw cooperated. Which he was now, and wasn't that more than a teensy bit suspicious? But *gift horse* and all that.

The captain slowed several feet from the Night Stealth. "Ms. Martin, that would not happen to be your *cow* boarding my vessel, by chance, would it?"

She took a step to the left, careful not to tread on the ends of the captain's wing feathers, and peered ahead. Sure enough, there was no mistaking the wide cow butt filling the entryway to the ship.

"Well, that's just great."

"Keep walking, Ms. Martin," the captain murmured over his shoulder as he picked up his pace again.

Oh, right. *Hop to it, Ava.*

She raised the stunner so it was pointing at him again. The clack of his boots on the ramp was swallowed up enough by the cavernous bay that the mechanics still seemed oblivious to their presence. But how was he going to get around May Belle?

The captain stopped. "Are you sure this creature is docile?"

"Pretty sure."

"All right." He placed his hands on May Belle's hipbones and leaned forward with a grunt.

"Moo." The cow ambled forward, bell dinging, until she was all the way inside the ship, leaving the doorway clear.

Yep, suspicious. She scurried up the ramp and into the corridor. "Well, that worked. Now how are we going to get her off?"

"We are not. We can put her in the holding cell for the duration." He bent closer, studying the wide bovine face. "Fascinating. She is very much like the Bezchian vava, only several hands smaller. And perfectly docile."

"We're taking her *with* us?" That was…well, not crazy, exactly. More like unexpected.

"Of course we are." He said it like it was just a given.

Okay, sure. Kidnap an alien cop, take a cow along, too. Made all the sense in the world.

He grasped the cow's halter and tugged. May Belle, being the good cow she'd been from the beginning, followed the captain straight into the glassed-in cell with an air of cud-chewing contentment.

Was all this too easy?

She stopped just outside the doorway. "What about food, and water?"

"It is my understanding that she has been eating since she arrived in the hangar bay." The captain stepped out of the room and tapped a few buttons. "But I just transferred the code for the simulated grain Doctor Kirla created. She should be fine."

The door slid closed with a soft shoosh. May Belle didn't even seem to notice. "Hmm. Well, she seems happy enough, for now."

"I set the controls so we can hear her in case she has any problems." He focused his guileless smile at her. "Now what?"

"Um…." She waved the stunner in the direction of the cockpit. "Go fly this thing?"

"I will fly, but you will sit with me in the cockpit." He brushed past her.

"You really didn't think I would leave you alone at this point, did you?"

The corners of his mouth twitched upward. "No."

God help her, but his lips were beautiful. Full, and made for kissing. How had no one ever put a ring on him?

He turned away, and she gave her head a shake.

Down, girl!

She trailed after him to the cockpit then claimed the co-pilot's seat. The headrest of the wing-friendly perch was set a foot higher than her head.

Sovah...*Captain Raptorclaw*...danced his fingers over the controls in front of him, and the mechanical whir of the ramp closing reached her ears. Then he gave her a sidelong look. "I will adjust the headrest for you, if you would like."

He could...but having him so close could lead to other things. "Just tell me how."

"You need your hands free to keep the stunner trained on me so I won't make any wrong moves, remember?"

She narrowed her eyes at him. Was this genuine cooperation or a trick? There was only one way to find out, and she did still have the stunner.

"Fine. Go ahead."

He leaned closer, locking his gaze with hers as he reached above her head. The subtle vanilla scent of him surrounded her, seeped deep into her senses. Her normal breathing became short, erratic pants. A faint beep came from somewhere above her head then he lowered the headrest until his forearms brushed her ears. And still, he didn't look away.

If her heart didn't stop pounding, it might explode out of her chest. She swallowed hard. God, his eyes were a starburst of deep, autumn orange and brown. The urge to kiss him for real threatened to override any common sense she had left. She flicked her gaze to his lips and back.

He leaned closer, brushed his lips over hers with the lightest touch, like a soft promise, then he moved back a short way. She followed him as if he was her magnet then caught herself before giving into her longing to smash her lips to his.

"How is that?" His words were a whisper of breath over her cheek.

"Good." So very good.

"Comfortable?"

"What?" Reality rushed back. *The headrest, genius, not the kiss.*

A slow grin curled his delicious lips. Yup. The headrest was fine, the kiss was fine, he was fine…if only there was time to explore other *fine things* about their current situation. But every moment they sat here widened the distance between her and her friends.

And since she'd probably passed the point of no return by kidnapping the captain… "We should go."

"Agreed." He moved all the way back into his seat… perch. "Strap down."

She eyed him and copied his moves as he shrugged into his safety harness. Then the sensation of floating sent the old, familiar flutter through her stomach. Outside the window, the hangar bay glided by as the ship turned to face the dark, star-speckled opening.

They were flying. In a spaceship.

"Mooo?"

"I second that, May Belle." *Breathe. In…out…in…out.*

The captain nodded. "I set the artificial gravity buffers and sealed the room. She will be fi—"

"*Bridge to Night Stealth.*" Rota's voice filled the cockpit.

Sovah tilted his head and fixed her with an expression of expectation. "I should answer that before they lockdown our only exit."

And her mission would be over before it began. "All right. Go ahead."

He tapped a button with one extended talon. "Captain Raptorclaw to Bridge. Need some quiet time, so I am taking her out for a routine patrol."

"*Understood, Captain. May a fair wind be under your wings. Bridge out.*"

Ava gaped at him. "Just like that? No questions?"

"I am *Axiom*'s captain."

"Uh…" And what exactly could she say to that? Especially since she knew next to nothing about the Protectorship, Bezchians, or aliens in general.

Off-worlders. Get it right.

The Night Stealth floated free of the larger ship, and the captain quirked his mouth in a half smile. "We are clear of *Axiom*. What is our course, Acting Night Stealth Captain?"

"Uh…" Yeah, her vocabulary had reverted to single-syllable teenager-level discourse.

She turned her gaze toward the view screen, and the sight

was spectacular as Captain Raptorclaw guided the ship around until *Axiom* was visible in front of them. And the stars…millions of them. Billions.

She drew in a sharp breath. "God Almighty."

Hey, three syllables, that time. How coherent of her.

"It gets better." Captain Raptorclaw said. "Wait until we get farther from *Axiom*."

"I-I don't know what to say about which way to go." She refocused her attention on him. "You said there was some way to trace your guy, officer. Can you still do that?"

"Yes, Captain." The clicking of his talons on the control board barely registered with her until the ship propelled forward and sailed over *Axiom*. "There. Found them."

"You did?" She whipped around, visually searching the screen for the gray's ship. "Where?"

"Not *them*, just Guan's signal." He was pressing more buttons now. "Course laid in, Captain."

The faint hum of something revving up—engines, maybe?—came from behind her, and a vibration tickled the soles of her slippered feet. "How did you figure it—"

"*Deputy Captain to Captain.*" Rota's voice cut her off. "*We detect the engagement of your light-drive engines.*"

"Hold onto your perch, Ms. Martin." He tapped a button, and the ship shot forward.

A yelp escaped her before she could stop it. The force of the launch pressed her backward, the support bar digging between her shoulder blades and along her spine. The pinpoints of starlight elongated then scattered into what resembled rolling geometric designs that looked a lot like what happened with a hard eye-rubbing.

Her stomach rolled right along with the distorted starlight. A long, low moan escaped through her mouth.

"First time is the worst." Funny how clear the captain's voice seemed.

"That's…comforting." Not. "Vomit bag?"

"You will not vomit."

"Wanna bet?" The damn man was grinning at her.

"It would not be fair of me to wager with you since I already know the outcome. Despite how you feel, no one has ever vomited launching into light-drive."

A deep heaving sound came from the detainment room.

She gave Sovah a narrow-eyed glare. "Hope you're right, 'cause that critter back there has four stomachs."

"She does?" Worry creases appeared across his feathered forehead and bracketed his mouth. He glanced over his shoulder…wing. Both.

"Yes, she does."

The pressure of the speed burst seemed to be easing now. Maybe he was right, and she wouldn't puke her guts out.

Sovah unclipped his harness. "I will check on your cow."

A surge of panic shot through her, and she reached out a hand. "Wait."

"What?"

"Um." How had her hand ended up clutching his thigh? His hard, muscular, warm thigh. "If you leave, who's going to fly this thing?"

The fabric of his uniform under her palm was softer than fleece and as smooth as silk.

A slow smile from him and, *boom*, every bit of common

sense evaporated from her brain, along with her name. Which was…something. What was wrong with her?

He closed his hands—which were also warm—around hers and raised them to his chest as he leaned close. Her body came to life and her breath hitched.

Kiss me again, you fool.

No, wait. Wasn't there a reason not to kiss him at all, ever?

Aw, screw it.

His lips grazed her ear, so warm and soft, and a sigh almost slipped out of her. "You can handle it for a moment, can you not?"

Sure, she could, as long as his lips…wait…. Had he really just whispered in her ear that *she* should fly the ship? Where were the sweet nothings that went along with the liquid heat running through her veins?

A burst of annoyance grounded her, and she pushed her hands against his chest. "Shove off, will ya?"

His bark of laughter filled the cockpit, and another zing of lust stabbed through her. "Not to worry, Ms. Martin, the ship will hold its course until told otherwise."

"Auto-pilot for space?" That could be handy info at some point.

"I suppose that is as good a name for it as any." He finally let go of her hands and slid off his perch. "I will check on our passenger now."

"Fine." She folded her arms in front of her and released an indignant huff. "You do that."

Alone, without her. Because seeing cow puke wasn't remotely on her bucket list. And also, so she could watch his fine ass as he sauntered down the hallway.

For a strident rule-follower, he sure didn't seem upset that she'd forced him out of his comfort-zone. So why was he here? It'd be the height of narcissism to believe it was just for *her*.

"Your May Belle is well." His voice drifted into the cockpit. "A little unstable on her feet, but no adverse effects."

"Well, thank God for that." She turned back to face the viewer.

The clomp of the captain's booted feet approached then he slid back into his seat. "No one has ever vomited, as I said."

"You sure did." She met his gaze and raised her chin a notch. "So, why are you being so cooperative, Captain Raptorclaw?"

TEN

Sovah considered the tiny, but not by any means fragile, Earthling female. "Sovah. My name is Sovah. Since you have shot me once already, we may as well dispense with formalities."

"All right, *Sovah*." She dipped her chin and raised the thin, twin arches of hair above her eyes. "Now, answer my questions."

Time for truth. "Because I want to save my people as much as you want to save yours."

She huffed. "Wouldn't have guessed that after the way you caved to Strauss the Louse."

"Yes." He slowly nodded. "I can understand why you would think so. But what captain worth their rank would turn down an opportunity to rescue their own crew?"

Or apprehend the grays' notorious bellwether.

"A pretty crappy one." She shook her head, the silver strands of her hair catching in the light above her. "Doesn't explain why you're doing this instead of hauling my butt in front of whatever justice system you have."

Because the mere thought of doing so triggered every protective instinct in him as never before. "After a career spent following orders, this is the first time I have found my given orders to be so repugnant. To challenge me in such a manner. Even my deputy captain recognized my quandary and took me to task."

"So, you and Rota set me up?"

"No. Not at all. Rota acted independently. When I realized what she, and you, had done, I made the conscious choice to go along with it. All in all, it is a solid plan, Ms. Martin."

A plan in which they both got what they wanted. She could return to her home world with her people without facing Alliance "justice." And he would return to Bezchi with his crew intact, his reputation in tatters, and possibly tagged as a traitor.

A small price to pay, in the end.

"But." Ava leaned forward. "As you pointed out, you *let* me shoot you."

"Yes." He turned his gaze to his lame wing in mock sorrow. "A calculated risk to test your commitment."

"You're an idiot, you know. What if I'd missed? Or accidently set the stunner too high and knocked you out?"

A rumble of laughter rolled through his chest. "Lucky for both of us, I keep *my* stunner on the lowest setting, which gives the recipient nothing more than a good shock. Do not crease your brow so, the wing is already recovered. See?"

He flexed it out as far as possible in the confined space.

She wrinkled her nose and shook her head. "Still a stupid thing to do. I mean, why bother when I could get arrested for this? And don't tell me there's no chance of that happening, because I've talked to your boss and he's got 'uptight asshole' written right across his feathered forehead."

"If that happens, I promise to visit you in prison." He could not resist teasing her.

"That's *so* comforting." She presented the stunner to him, grip first. "You can have this back now."

He extended his arm, and she placed the device in his palm, her fingers lingering a wing-flutter longer than necessary. There was no question their attraction for each other was mutual, and they should talk about it at some point.

But not now. He slipped the stunner back into its holster at his hip. "Thank you, Ms. Martin."

"Ava." She leaned back on her perch. "Since we're forgoing formalities and all now."

"Ava." Her given name was like a sigh of peace. "Does it have a meaning?"

She snorted. "It means bird. Apparently, I was almost constantly flitting around in utero, so my mom called me her little bird. When I turned out to be a girl, she chose Ava. Dad wanted to name me Marie, so that became my middle name instead. And a bit of a family joke."

"I do not understand. What is the joke?"

"It's complicated to explain, but there's a saint on Earth, and sometimes when people pray to her, they say Avé Maria. Which sort of sounds like Ava Marie."

"I see." Not really. *Ah-vey* sounded different than *A-vah*.

Without deeper reference, understanding flew by him. He offered up a lopsided courtesy grin anyway.

Her laugh brightened the atmosphere in the cockpit. "I guess you had to be there."

"Perhaps so. But your name is quite beautiful."

"Thank you, Sovah." Her expression softened and pleasure shone in her eyes. "Now it's your turn. What's your name mean? And why do so many people aboard your ship have the same last name? Are you all related, or something?"

"Raptorclaw is my clan's name. Many races, like yours, use a surname that is particular to their family unit. But on Bezchi we are identified by our clan. There are four—five including the phoenix elders, but they are different. Raptorclaw, Landwalker, Waterdiver, Rockdweller, and Firewing." This was not going to make any more sense to her than Avé Maria did to him. "Sovah means night."

It was not exactly unnerving the way she gazed straight into his eyes, as though searching for his soul. More like pleasurable in an anticipatory way.

Finally, she nodded. "Your eyes remind me of an owl's, a nocturnal bird on Earth."

And hers were the color of the sky at the height of a summer day. Opposite, yet reflective of each other. A sense of predestination washed over him. His future and hers, together. Entwined. Could it be?

He gave himself a mental shake. Wishful poetic notions were for dreamers, not for old Protectorship captains. "Tell me about your fellow abductees. You must have been together for a long time to have forged such close ties that you would risk so much to save them."

"It was only a week, but May Belle and two other humans had been there at least a week longer than Regina and I." She shrugged her shoulders. "You know what they say about bonding over shared traumatic experiences."

He did, had even experienced such connections himself, but something in her tone seemed evasive. Yet, who was he to judge when he had withheld his own personal reasons behind a lifetime of actions? Or inactions.

Ava cleared her throat. "Um, so, how long do you think it'll take to catch up with the grays?"

"It depends on the speed of their travel. They will slow once they believe they are not being pursued by *Axiom*, but there is no telling when they will reach that level of comfort." He turned his attention to the console. "See this blinking light? That is a signal from the internal tracer of the commander of my sentinels, who is aboard the grays' cargo vessel."

"Does everyone have a *tracer*?" The inflection on the last word held a tinge of disgust.

"Only those in military and law-enforcement types of service. And the tracers are removed from our arms at the end of their service."

"They're temporary, then?"

"Yes." He turned to face her fully. "We do not intrude on the privacy of our citizens, but we do everything we can to keep those protecting us and the Alliance of Planets safe."

She met his gaze straight on then darted her tongue out over her lips. "Thank you for keeping me safe."

Was he keeping her safe? Safe would have been locking her into her quarters aboard *Axiom* and following orders. On the other wing, there was a rightness in being here with her. Something deeper than the opportunity to know her better…although there was no denying the desire burning inside him to learn everything about her.

"You are welcome." He leaned his spine against the narrow back support bar. "I am curious, how did the grays lure you in, Ava?"

A sardonic laugh bubbled out of her at his question. "Remember when I said I thought they'd been abducting humans for centuries? The more I've thought about it, the more convinced I am that it's true. And that they know us humans pretty damn well."

Uncomfortably well. And probably the cows, too.

She launched into her trip to Vegas, why and with whom. About barely being able to keep her eyes open as she drove through the dark desert night. Then the miracle of coming across the so-called motel, only to have it turn out to be one of the grays' pick-up ships in disguise.

"Talk about a rude awakening. Literally." She gave her head a shake. "Until that moment, I was a card-carrying member of the UFOs-and-little-green-men-don't-exist club. Or tall gray men in this case. But that's what I mean by they know us. Why else would they plunk down a fake motel on a long, empty stretch of highway in the middle of god-awful nowhere? Because humans need sleep, especially when they're traveling at night."

He nodded slowly, the unfocused distance of contemplation in his eyes. "I am very disappointed that Protectorship Command does not seem to be aware of the problem, or even your planet. You must be from an unexplored section of the galaxy…and while there are many of those, it still concerns me."

It shouldn't have been surprising that his Alliance of Planets hadn't explored every nook and cranny; the Milky Way was a large place. A hell of a lot larger than she'd ever been able to wrap her head around.

He returned his full attention to her. "I am sorry, Ava."

"For what? Not stopping this from happening? Pfft." She made a swiping gesture with one hand. "You said it yourself, the Alliance probably doesn't know about Earth. And you can't be *everywhere* saving *everyone* now, can you?"

He caught her hand and gently cradled it between his. "It is our duty to protect so you do not miss out on special life celebrations."

"But—"

"Do you have family on Earth?"

"Yes. My niece, Robyn, and her kids." Of the family members who were still alive, Robyn was the only one left who hadn't deserted her years ago.

"How must they feel about your disappearance?"

Robyn and the kids would be upset. Robyn's husband, Kevin…not so much.

Sovah nodded as if he'd guessed her thoughts. "That is why I have dedicated my life to the Protectorship."

"You lost someone to the grays?" The thought sent an ache stabbing through her heart.

"No, they have not targeted Bezchi for generations. We are too big, and fight nasty." He caressed the back of her hand, callouses rough over her suddenly too-sensitive skin.

"But even as a fledgling, I heard of them hitting other planets, and it never sat right with me."

A man with a heart, then. A big, giving, idealistic heart. "Are you, like, a police officer, or military?"

He paused the stroking and tipped his head to one side in a rather owlish manner. "Po-liss?"

"Someone sworn to serve and protect ordinary folks, but not fight in wars."

"Ah, yes. Po-liss fits. The Alliance military does not do much except train for potential combat situations."

"That's *it*?"

"Not exactly." He grinned and moved his fingers up her forearm then back to her wrist, leaving a decadent trail of goosebumps across her skin. "They also serve Alliance government officials in the same capacity as we serve civilians."

"So." She cleared her throat to distract herself from the sudden lack of clarity in her brain…and the tendrils of heat snaking through her veins. "It sounds like there's a bit of a friendly rivalry between the branches of service."

"I cannot confirm nor deny the possibility." His amber gaze looked more like hot coals in a campfire. "Ava, I—"

She reached out her free hand and cupped her palm over his cheek. "We're both old enough not to beat around the bush, Sovah."

By his puzzled gaze, it was obvious the saying was unfamiliar to him, but then he raised her wrist and pressed a kiss to the delicate skin. "The way your pulse flutters against my lips, I am coming to realize that I might have had ulterior motives with you all along."

The heat flared into an all-consuming flame. Ulterior motives were exactly what she had in mind, too. She pushed off her perch, moving to hover just far enough to look down at him. His gaze stayed with hers, and warm puffs of his breath skittered over the skin exposed at the V of her PJ top.

Devil-may-care daring filled her. Could they be interrupted at any time by catching up with the grays? Sure. Or, maybe not. It all depended how soon the grays hit their comfort zone. But even a little taste of this alien...*offworlder*...would be better than nothing. She flicked her gaze down to his lips then back up. Would he understand her unspoken question?

He raised his chin ever so slightly. That was answer enough. She leaned in, closing the remaining distance, claiming his mouth, thrusting her tongue between his parted lips. The heavy warmth of his large, square hands moved up and down her back, pulling her close until her breasts were fully pressed against his chest.

A long, low moan of pleasure rolled from her. Then her world tilted as Sovah's grip around her tightened and he pushed off the perch, his long stride moving them down the hall toward the back of the ship. She wrapped her legs around his hips, clinging to him, swirling her tongue around his until—

"*Oomph.*"

Oh, mercy. He had pinned her back up against a cool, smooth surface and was conducting a thorough investigation of her neck, her shoulder, her breasts—with his lips. Huh. When had the buttons of her PJs come undone?

She pushed her chest forward. "You missed a spot, Captain." Or two.

A deep growl rumbled from him and he ran his tongue round one nipple, warm and wet. She dug her fingernails into his shoulders, arching her head back.

"Sovah." The last syllable of his name came out as a sigh.

He drew her in so hard the sensation zinged straight down between her legs and a groan welled up from the depths of her. This. She wanted all of this, of him. Had waited her entire life for this feeling of rightness, and now that it was within her reach, she'd be an idiot to let it slip away.

"Mooo?"

Guess the smooth surface against her back was the glass of the holding cell. May Belle was getting an eyeful, for sure. Well, in for a penny, in for a pound. Now to figure out how compatible Bezchians were to humans. She wiggled one hand down between them, under his shirt until her fingers snagged on the waistband of his pants…and praise be, he went commando! She closed her fingers around the hard, hot velvet of his shaft. Definitely the right shape, though a bit longer and thicker than most human men. But no worries there.

"Ava," he groaned as he pushed his hips forward, sliding within her grip.

The look in his hooded gaze was part wild predator, and all sexy in a primitive sort of way. When was the last time a guy had looked at her like that? Never. No guy ever had. Sure, they'd gazed on her with desire, dominance, or lust, and a couple maybe even with love. But Sovah's gaze was different; binding, in a way, but not alpha-possessive. She would be free to walk away from this at any point, without consequence. But did she want to?

Not. At. All.

Buzz, buzz, buzz!

The ship's alarm shattered the sexually charged tension around them faster than a cold shower.

She blinked up at him. "Uh. Is that a bad alarm?"

"For our interlude, yes." He leaned forward, bowing his shoulders until his forehead rested against hers. "On the other wing, that is a proximity alert and could mean the bellwether has finally stopped."

A soft laugh escaped her. "Their timing sucks."

"It is disappointing, for certain." He grinned. "I will need my...*part* back, Ava."

Oh, right. She released his still-hard cock and withdrew her hand. "Rain check? That's English for, let's pick up where we left off later."

"I would like that *very* much."

He rebuttoned her PJ top then draped his arm over her shoulders and walked her back to the bridge. Once there, he retrieved her slippers from under his perch and handed them to her before taking his seat. His transformation from potential lover back to Protectorship captain seemed almost seamless, except for a couple of micro-shifts he made to *adjust* himself on the perch. Other than that, the mantle of leadership settled around him as effortlessly as it was for her to slide her feet back into her slippers. Second nature. Which was why he was the captain, obviously.

He grinned up at her. "We found them."

A shot of excitement zinged through her. "Awesome."

We. He said *we*. It was that easy for him to include her, and refreshing after a career laden with egocentrics—male and female—who often forgot they weren't the glorious center of the universe.

She slid into the co-pilot's seat and directed her gaze to the blurred stars on the screen. "So? Where are they?"

"Not visible yet." He finger-punched a couple of buttons. "But they will be soon. I have engaged stealth mode so they will not see us drop out of light-drive. Safety harness, if you please, Ava."

"Is stopping as bad as starting?" She pulled the straps around her and slid the clips into place, the satisfying clicks reassuring her that if things got rough, she wasn't going anywhere.

"I hope not."

A small snort escaped her. "*That's* comforting."

He gave her an apologetic look. "You are the first Earthling I have ever encountered in this situation. But you did not vomit before, so there is hope."

"True."

"It is your cow that worries me." He turned his head far enough to look back down the hallway. "Prepare yourself, May Belle. Disengaging light-drive in three…two…one."

Her body pushed forward against the restraints as the endlessly rotating curvilinear streaks of light contracted back into glittering stars in the blackness of space, and a jabbing headache sucker-punched her right behind her eyes.

"Nuugh."

"Ava?" The comforting weight of Sovah's hand rested on her shoulder.

She pressed her thumb and forefinger over the bridge of her nose. "Headache."

"A physical reaction to the abrupt speed change." He moved his hand to cap the top of her head and warmth seeped through her scalp. "This does happen sometimes, even with the dampeners."

"It's getting better already." She tipped her head back against the headrest and met his gaze. "A scalp massage would probably help."

Hint, hint.

Sympathetic mirth sparkled in his eyes, and he kneaded his fingers over her hair. "While I do this, take a look at the view screen."

She shifted her gaze forward. All the stars were still there, but two of them seemed out of place. Closer, less bright, almost shadowy. "Is that them?"

"Yes."

"And they can't see us, right?"

"Not at all."

"Wow." Off-worlder technology was so cool. "So, what's the plan?"

"The bellwether is most likely preparing to take the cargo vessel aboard. We will attach to the underside of the cargo vessel and go aboard with them."

"Um." She gave him her full attention. "And how will we get out again?"

He shifted his gaze to the screen, pressed his lips together, and frowned.

"Sovah, please tell me you're not making this up as we

go along." The distance between them and the cargo ship had closed…a lot.

"I am not. What happens next depends upon what the grays do once their cargo vessel is safely stowed in their hangar." He danced the long fingers of his free hand over the controls, all the while scritching her head with the other. "And there is only one way to find that out."

"By going in."

"Exactly. Look." He released her head and pointed in the direction of the bellwether. "They are opening the hangar to take in the cargo vessel now."

Sure enough, a long rectangle of glowing light had appeared along the edge of the disc-shaped ship. And it was growing wider. "Are we going to make it?"

"Without a doubt." Sovah leaned forward a fraction, watching the screen as the distance between them and the cargo ship holding her friends shrank. "Almost…there…"

She tightened her fingers around the cushioned edges of her perch and shifted her gaze back to Sovah's capable hands at the controls. Good thing one of them seemed confident about pulling this off.

ELEVEN

Sovah guided the Night Stealth into position under the boxy cargo vessel. It barely made the softest thump as the above-board magnetic clamps connected to the underside. If anyone inside the grays' small vessel heard the sound, they should dismiss it as routine structural noise caused by being dragged through space by a tractor beam for so long.

"Attachment procedure complete." Smooth as a youngling's downy wings.

Ava breathed out as if she had been holding her breath. "So, now what?"

"Now, we wait as the bellwether guides it in. After that, we will see."

"Oh, so you *are* winging it." She rolled her eyes, but this time there was a hint of dry humor in their clear blue depths.

"Somehow, that reference makes some sort of sense." He allowed a small grin. "Thank you for trusting me."

She laughed. "Hey, you've boarded more pirate ships than I have. Besides, at this point, I'm finally willing to admit that all this is way beyond my control."

The warm glow around his heart expanded. It took great inner strength to recognize one's lack of experience and step aside as she was. He held her gaze for a moment longer, then refocused on powering down everything except artificial gravity and life-support. Hopefully he would have something of a plan for what came next before they arrived. Anything less would be a betrayal of her trust.

Ten minutes later, the cargo vessel rested on the shiny white metal deck of the hangar bay. And still, no ideas had come to him. What he needed was intel.

"Visual, pan bay." The view screen image moved, revealing each section of the hangar deck in sequence from starboard to port. Not a gray in sight yet. But the docking crew would arrive as soon as the hangar was repressurized.

Ava leaned forward against her restraints. "Where is everyo—"

Mammoth-sized doors on the port side of the bay parted slowly to reveal a group of at least thirty grays armed with prods. "There they are. Here to unload the *merchandise*."

The word left a coat of bitterness on his tongue.

"Bastards." Ava mumbled the word like it was a curse, which it might be in her language. "What are we going to do?"

"Wait for an opportunity." He met her gaze. "Which could happen when we least expect it, so stay alert and be ready to follow my command."

Her eyes narrowed. "Don't even *think* about leaving me here."

"Ava—"

"*No.*" She turned in her seat to face him. "I still need to be in control of *something* here, Captain. And I am not one of your soldiers to be ordered around."

A fact of which he was well aware. "You are a civilian, and my job is to protect you."

"Screw you, Robo-cop. You're going to need m—"

BOOM!

The Night Stealth shuddered, and a yelp of surprise came from Ava.

BOOM! BOOM! BOOM! BOOM!

What in the fiery blazes is happening?

He peered at the view screen. Flashes of light preceded each explosion, equipment on the deck sparked and smoldered—or at least what was left of it did—and the grays who were not lying motionless were seeking cover or pounding at the now-closed door they had marched through moments ago. The hangar bay was in turmoil.

"Mooooooo." Even May Belle's distress over the situation was clear.

But what *was* the situation?

A dark figure arrowed into view through the air, a blur dropping onto a fleeing gray. Then another, and another, and three more. "Blessed fair air currents. My crew is *attacking* them."

Had they managed to retake the cargo vessel? If so, how?

Ava gasped. "*Look*. That's Axill running down the ramp, and…well, shit, *Regina*? That's Regina, and a bunch of others who were abducted!"

She was right, a civilian mob was charging into the fray. Every last one of them were armed with stunners and blasters. But *how*? That was completely against regulations.

And what I have done is any better?

Leading one civilian, or many, into danger did not matter. But what was done was done.

He gave his wrist comm a quick tap. "Sentry Commander Guan."

"*Captain?*" Mild surprise filtered through in Guan's tinny voice.

"Yes, it is me. What is happening out there?"

"*We regained full control of the cargo vessel in transit, Captain, and the bellwether had no idea.*" Guan's voice filled the cockpit. "*We targeted their main power source with a pulse blast. At least two-thirds of the bellwether is disabled, and the best escape they can manage is sub-light speed. If you hurry, it should be a simple matter for Axiom to net them.*"

That was quick thinking on Guan's part. Enough to earn a commendation. "We are aboard the Night Stealth, attached to the underbelly of the cargo vessel."

"*I thought I heard something clamp—*"

"Why are there armed civilians on the deck, Guan?"

"*Earthlings.*" It sounded like the commander had pushed the frustration-laden word through clenched teeth.

A snort-cough came from Ava's direction, and he fought the urge to give her a side-long glare. On the positive, the grays had not decompressed the hangar and spaced them all yet, which verified Guan's report that the bellwether was severely disabled.

"I am going out there." He unfastened his harness and slid from his perch. "Stay here, Ava."

"No way." She had her harness retracted before the words were fully out of her mouth.

"I do not have—"

"*Listen to me*! I've been shooting since I was eight, and hunting with a rifle since I was twelve to put food on my family's table."

"Yet, how many sentient beings have you shot?"

Her blue eyes glittered with challenge. "Two."

He blinked at her. That was unexpected.

"First one when I was thirteen and my older cousin tried to rape me. I shot him in the thigh. The second was some random guy who tried to drag me into an alley in New York City. I disarmed him and used his gun on him. Let's just say that it didn't have a stun setting." She shrugged. "I'm not afraid to hurt someone to defend myself."

Clearly. And like an idiot, he had underestimated her. "This is a battle situation."

"And the alley wasn't?"

Fair point. "Come with me, then."

He strode out of the cockpit, not waiting to see if she would follow. She would. He paused halfway to May Belle's holding area and tapped a code into the keypad for the Night Stealth's arsenal. The panel slid open with a soft *shoosh*, revealing the special stash of weaponry stored behind it. Weapons designed with a kill setting.

"Pick one that might work for you. Quickly."

Her gaze darted over the munitions then she pointed. "That one."

"A disruptor." He disengaged the storage lock, lifted it out, then fiddled with the settings. "It is on maximum stun."

At the sound of her wordless protest, he raised one finger. "It will incapacitate a gray for at least half a day, and I want as many of them alive as possible for questioning and to face charges."

She nodded, and pride welled in him. This small, wingless female was the epitome of bravery.

He held up the weapon, pointing to each part. "Trigger, muzzle. Please do not aim it at anyone who is not a gray. Like me, for instance."

Her sudden grin was as brilliant as it was mischievous. "Don't piss me off."

A laugh erupted from deep inside him. He leaned close to her. "Would it piss you off if I kissed you now?"

"It would piss me off if you didn't."

Ah, she did not mince words. He extended the disruptor to her then closed the space between them to claim her mouth with his. For a kiss only involving lips and no tongue, it was like a vortex, threatening to drag him in. If only there was time.

With a force of will, he drew back slowly, meeting her glassy-eyed gaze. "Be careful, yes?"

"Yes." She nodded. "You too, sweet cheeks."

"I will." For her, he would promise never to die, even though they both knew better. He grasped a larger weapon and gave the locking mechanism a quick finger flick. It came to life with a faint whine. "Time to go."

The moment the Stealth's door opened, the shouts and sounds of the battle outside assaulted Ava's ears. She stepped up next to Sovah in the doorway, and a wave of nausea crashed over her.

Breathe. Don't let him know how much heights affect me.

Thirty feet below, humans and humanoids were fanned out, taking on grays like it was a barroom brawl. A flash of bright yellow caught her attention just in time to see Regina karate kick a gray in the nuts with his spike-heeled boot. Nearby, Axill threw punches like the Nordic god he portrayed on the big screen. He was actually quite glorious, for a kid.

Then, the scene was blocked by mottled white and gray feathers. Sovah had surrounded her with his wings. "Fire from here, you will have a better view. Use the hatchway for protection if someone shoots back. The hull will absorb the shots."

"What about the ramp?" She had to shout to hear her own words.

"I am not lowering it yet. You will not stand a feather's chance in the wind if the grays rush it."

"Good point. What about you?"

He grinned down at her, retracted his wings, stepped backward, then plummeted over the edge and out of sight.

A gasp escaped her; the sound lost in the din.

He jumped! He fucking jumped!

The guy so worried about her getting hurt was now hurtling toward the unforgiving metal floor. No wait, his wings were open, and he was soaring, his trajectory arcing upward and just clearing the edge of the cargo ship, firing at a group of three grays hunched behind some sort of machinery. And he laid out every damn one of them.

107

Impressive.

Thud!

Something hit the side of the ship inches from her. She ducked to one side then peeked around the door frame. A lone gray stood on the floor, legs wide with its gun pointed up at her. She jerked back just as another pulse blew past her and hit the interior ceiling of the hallway. A few sparks showered down, and thankfully extinguished before hitting the floor.

"Mooo."

"It's all right, May Belle." Poor thing. All the loud noises must've been discombobulating for a creature used to grazing in quiet fields all day. "Once this is over, we'll go find Nora and Axill."

If they survived. "All right, you pasty little a-hole. This is for ruining my Vegas trip."

She stepped forward—not too close to the edge—then tapped the disruptor's trigger over and over. The gray jerked back, its expression going from gritty battle-snarl to wide-eyed shock. Its legs folded as its gun slid from its long fingers then it was on the floor, convulsing.

"Gotcha."

She twisted back behind the shelter of the wall. But was he *down* down?

Should be since at least four of her five shots had hit him. She leaned forward to peer around the doorway. The gray lay spread-eagle and unmoving on the ground. Okay, now that she had a better idea how the disruptor worked, she was ready for more action.

"All right. Who's next?" Her gaze latched onto a flash of yellow below. "*Reg*, over here!"

Her friend moved his head from side to side then up. It was obvious the moment he saw her because his eyes widened comically. The drag queen altered course in her direction, followed by two grays. She raised the disruptor then lined them up in her sights.

"A little closer…a little… There." She tapped the trigger once, twice, and the grays went down hard, one sliding across the floor into the other. "Eat lead, bastards."

Or pulse beams, or whatever.

Regina's whoop drew her attention. "Honey, where have you *been*?"

A wave of dizziness washed over her. Whoa, yeah. Not liking being so close to the edge of the door.

"Oh, you know. Here and there." She lowered the muzzle of her gun and wrapped her free hand around the edge of the doorway as her friend came to a stop below. "How, Regina? How do you run in those boots?"

"Practice, darling." Regina's grin was droll, but there was a sparkle in his dark eyes. "I'd offer to bring you some more targets, but I think we're almost finished here. That, and the god-like screen-star would be pissed if I interrupted his fun."

Thirty yards away, Axill KOed the last gray standing in front of him. *Ooh, nice shot.*

She scanned the area nearby. "Where's Nora?"

"Still on the ship, doing the librarian thing," Reg replied.

"Uh, what's that mean?"

Reg shrugged. "Distracting the kids by reading to them."

"*Books?*"

"Honey, that woman is pure tenacity packed into a tiny body. After we took the ship back, she found her damn e-reader in storage and coerced one of the Bezchians into recharging it."

A laugh burst out of her at the visual of little Nora going up against a towering Bezchian. And winning.

Regina sniffed, making a show of inspecting the nails of his left hand. "It helped that she had a superhero backing her up. Axill is not batting for my team, in case you're wondering."

She wasn't. "Will you survive the disappointment?"

"I suppose." Reg dragged out the O. "It would be harder if not for the Bezchians. Gotta love a race who has specially designed straps they wear when flying. They call them flying *leathers*."

"I didn't know about this."

"Guan explained it to me."

"Guan?"

Reg met her gaze pointedly. "What happens in space, stays in space, honey. Are you coming down from there anytime soon? It looks like you're standing in midair. It's disconcerting."

"Well...." It did sound like the fighting had settled down, and none of the grays were standing, or even conscious anymore.

A fluid motion caught her gaze. Sovah was jogging across the hangar floor, heading in her direction. He picked up his pace then pumped his wings and floated off the floor as though he was filled with helium. Her breath hitched in her chest as he rose higher with each wing beat.

It's like watching an angel fly.

And then he was there. She took a few steps back to make room for him to land. Reaching out to touch him was so natural, so right. "You're back."

Obviously.

He brushed her hair back and hooked it behind her ear. "Are you unharmed, Ava?"

"Yes...no." Oh, hell. Way to sound like a simpleton.

She closed her hands over the fabric of his uniform shirt and dragged him down for a kiss. It was hard, and a bit desperate on her part, but it also grounded her in a reality that didn't include the thirty-foot drop-off to her left.

Sovah pulled back first, his gaze intense. "I am needed aboard the cargo vessel, but I did not wish to leave you here alone."

"Newsflash, you're not leaving me here again."

"Do I look like I have a desire to ascend to the Great Aerie anytime soon?"

"Well..." A mischievous grin curved his mouth then he bent and suddenly she was cradled in his arms. "Sovah? What are you *doing*?"

"Taking you to the cargo ship." He stepped toward the ledge.

"No, wait...the ramp. Oh, *fuuuu....*"

The damn man jumped, and the stomach-wrenching feeling of free-fall tore a scream from her throat.

TWELVE

Sovah coved his wings, slowing his decent to the base of the cargo vessel's ramp.

"Almost there, *viché*." He murmured the soothing words, grazing his lips over the shell of Ava's ear.

His little Earthling did not respond. Nor did she loosen the wads of his uniform fabric clutched tightly in her closed fists. And her face remained pressed against his shoulder, eyes squeezed shut. Almost as if she did not like to fly.

He angled his body and glided feet first to a gentle landing. Still no response from her. Should he tell her they had arrived? Put an end to the pleasant weight of her in his arms? Or the warmth of her breath against his skin?

No.

Besides, she did not seem inclined to disengage either. He strode up the vessel's ramp, turning his body sideways to fit them both through the hatchway then followed the corridor in the direction of the bridge.

Halfway there, the tension in Ava's body eased a bit and she raised her head. "What's going on?"

"We are meeting with my officers. Sentry Commander Guan has some explaining to do, and we need a plan."

There was no telling when *Axiom* would arrive, but arrive it would. Rota was no more likely to squander an opportunity to apprehend the bellwether than he was. If only there was a way to contact her without risking alerting the grays to the imminent arrival of the law. The last thing Rota needed was to drop out of light-drive to a barrage of pulse-fire.

"Put me down." The soft slap of Ava's palm against his chest was enough to refocus his attention to her. "I can walk."

He stopped and lowered her feet to the ground but did not release her from his embrace. "What is bothering you, Ava?"

Was that anger flashing in her eyes, or extreme annoyance?

Her lips thinned. "I. Hate. Flying."

Anger, then. That explained her reactions. "I did not realize."

"Obviously." She pushed away from him, and he released her. "Lead the way, Captain."

So, he had been demoted back to his title. He gave her a curt nod and moved in the direction of their destination. Moments later, he stepped onto the bridge, Ava in his wake. There were far more beings present in the command center than just his crew, and several eyed him with unabashed curiosity. Especially the yellow-clad warrior-male leaning against the backrest of the captain's perch behind Commander Guan.

"Ava!" A short, bespectacled Earthling female stood to the left of the door. She released the hand of another warrior-male, this one with long, blond hair, and embraced his little Earthling. "I'm so glad you're safe."

"You okay, Nora?" There was a hint of motherly concern in Ava's question. She cared about these people.

"Fine. We're all fine." Nora stepped back. "But May Belle wandered off, and Axill and I haven't been able to find her."

"She's in the ship Sovah and I came in, don't worry. She's fine."

Guan rose from the perch, and the yellow-clad Earthling moved back, suddenly more interested in the... Was that a cap of long, flowing white hair in his hand?

"Captain." Guan touched two fingers to the point of his headfeathers in greeting.

"Sentry Commander." He returned the salute. "How did the grays take back control of the cargo vessel after I left? And how did the bellwether locate it?"

"After you disengaged the docking tube, the grays stormed the bridge. We had no chance to alert *Axiom* before they had us in custody and regained control. After that, the grays sent out a coded locator transmission to their bellwether. Regina," he waved his hand in the direction of the yellow-clad human warrior, who fluttered his fingers in greeting, "was able to evade recapture, and released us from the cargo holds. We took back control of the vessel shortly after their bellwether tractored it from *Axiom*. It seemed the perfect opportunity for *Axiom* to capture both ships, so I activated my tracer, and we made no attempts to break free. It would reflect poorly on us if we let a vessel full of civilians be blasted right after we had rescued them."

"Yet you risked the same civilians by allowing them to go into hand-to-hand combat with the grays. What in the name of the wide-open skies were you thinking?"

Guan compressed his lips into a thin line and visibly swallowed.

"It wasn't like we gave him a choice." The yellow warrior, Regina, slipped the hair cap on his head then stepped around the perch to stand with Guan. "We humans don't like taking no for an answer. Not easily, at least."

One corner of Guan's mouth twitch upward for a moment. "They were very...persuasive, Captain."

So it would seem. "Persuasive enough to have you abandon your oath?"

"Honey." Regina made a bobbling motion with his head, which somehow did not dislodge the hair cap. "He didn't see us coming. Oh, he ordered us to stay inside, all right, even after we helped take the ship back. I think these good officers of yours have learned not to underestimate us again, and you shouldn't either."

Given his experiences with Ava, that was probably true. "You represent the prisoners, then?"

"If you're asking if I instigated all this, no." He extended one graceful hand. "I'm Regina Gardenia, but call me Reg. And you are the fabulous Captain Raptorclaw, I presume?"

Fabulous? What had his crew said about him? "I am Captain Raptorclaw."

"Charmed." Regina raised his eyebrows and wiggled his fingers with some undefinable expectation.

Sovah frowned at the proffered appendage. Exactly what was the Earthling doing? He gave the colorful human a brief nod before turning his attention back to Guan. "You disabled the bellwether, how?"

In the periphery of his vision, he noted Regina lowering his hand with a small huff.

"We sent a series of energy pulses into the bellwether's command center via conduits. They may be able to limp away, but they will not get far, and they certainly will not escape *Axiom*."

"That was a tactically sound maneuver, Commander."

"Thank you, Captain."

The one called Axill grunted. "Great. Now we can talk about getting everyone home?"

"Not without May Belle." Nora gazed up at the male with wide, pleading eyes.

Axill patted her hand where it rested on his arm. "Of course, not without her, Nor-Nor."

Right. Returning the Earthlings to their planet must be a priority over the Alliance citizens, as they were the most displaced. He glanced at Ava. Her gaze was focused on the couple, and a small, knowing smile played on her lips. Something in his heart twisted in pain. How could he let her go when that was the last thing in the universe he wanted?

Her safety, and her family are my priority.

Her niece would be bereft at her disappearance—her friends, as well. There would be no legal recourse for her if she stayed with him. And he, of course, would not escape his responsibility in disobeying a direct command. Chief Commissioner Strauss was not a very forgiving person when crossed.

Sorrow twisted in his chest. The only guaranteed way to

protect her was to send her home where no one could touch her.

Besides, all the civilians must be off the bellwether before *Axiom* arrived. The grays might not give up their vessel easily. The possibility of a battle existed, and even if Ava did not have family and friends back on Earth, he would not—could not—risk her life.

He glided his fingertips over the skin of his inner forearm, giving the subdermal tracer three taps to activate it, then refocused his attention onto Guan. "Sentry Commander, disengage your tracer, then prepare to return the civilians to their planets of origin. *Axiom* should be enroute to intercept, and can follow my signal."

"Yes, Captain."

"Start with Earth's citizens. The coordinates to their home world must be in this vessel's data banks." It would be a little inconvenient for the Alliance citizens, but they would get home in due time.

Ava jerked her head around. "Wait, what about *you*?"

"If I leave the bellwether, *Axiom* will follow my signal and we will lose the best chance we have ever had to capture them."

"So, you're staying." It was not a question.

"I must."

"Well." Her raised chin proclaimed her stubbornness. "I'm staying with you, then."

Her words wrapped around his heart. If only she could. "No."

"No? *No*?" She stepped in front of him and poked him in the chest with one finger. "I'm a grown-ass woman, Sovah. I don't need your permission."

"Maybe not. But I will not allow the Protectorship to find a way to bring you up on charges that would put you in prison for the remainder of your life, either. You must return to your planet where they cannot touch you."

Regina made a low whistling sound. "Sugar, what the hell did you *do*?"

Ava waved her hand in Sovah's direction. "I kidnapped him. And…stole his ship."

Even though they both knew there was more to it than that, it was clear she recognized exactly how Protectorship Command would interpret the events that had led them to this moment.

He turned his attention back to Guan. The poor male's eyes bulged with shock. "Send someone to move the Night Stealth to the hangar deck, and retrieve the Earth cow from the detainment cell. She will be much happier to have her hooves on her home planet."

"Yes, Captain."

"Ava, a moment of your time?"

"Oh, sure. Why not?" She turned away and stomped off the bridge, her anger a palpable cloud around her.

Ava stopped at what appeared to be the same intersection of hallways where she'd first plowed into Sovah. It seemed like ages ago, not less than a day.

She pivoted around to face him. "Can't we just tell your command I was set up?"

"Do you wish to risk Rota's career? Her family?"

Shame surged through her. "No." How could she be so selfish? Rota had given them a shot at rescuing the crew, capturing the bellwether, and maybe, just maybe, getting her and her friends home. "So, just like that, you're sending me back. Doesn't matter what I think, or how I feel."

"It does matter. *You* matter. And that is another reason you cannot stay." There was a bleakness in his expression, as if he was willing her to understand.

A flutter of fear danced in her gut. "What's going on, Sovah? Why is it so important to you that I leave?"

One corner of his mouth ticked sideways. "If *Axiom* secures the bellwether without incident, I will be brigged for the remainder of the cruise back to Bezchi, where I will be brought before a Protectorship tribunal for questioning. I do not expect that to go in my favor. On the other wing, should *Axiom* fail to take the bellwether, they will destroy it."

Why did that even matter? It wasn't like any of them would still be... "Oh. Wait...*with you still aboard?*"

He didn't answer, didn't have to. The truth was in his eyes. His future was either prison, or death. There was no *them* in either one of those scenarios.

Shit. This wasn't how things were supposed to turn out. But, this was his job, his calling, who'd he been long before she'd come into his life, and to argue would be like telling him none of that mattered. It did, though, in the same way she mattered to him.

All hints of anger drained out of her, leaving her with no fuel to rail at him, or at life in general. Sometimes, the *greater good* sucked.

"I do not want it to be, but I see no other path." The agony laced through his words was a reflection of what was in her heart.

At least I know he feels the same way.

Didn't make things any easier, though. She stepped in close, wrapped her arms around his middle, and rested her head against his chest. His scent surrounded her as the rhythmic thump of his heart beat under her ear. "For what it's worth, I'd really appreciate it if you didn't martyr yourself."

He folded his arms around her and pulled her closer. "I heartily agree with that, and will do my best."

"Thank you, for everything, Sovah. I will never forget."

"Nor will I." A rustle reached her ears as he shrouded them in his wings, like a shield holding back reality, if only for a moment longer. "You have my heart, viché."

Treasure. He had called her that earlier, as he'd carried her from the Night Stealth—

"*Captain.*" The voice came from his wristband. Reality had found them again.

"Yes, Security Commander."

"*The cow has been secured aboard. We await you on the bridge.*"

"On my way."

She loosened her hold on him, took a step back, and met his gaze. The feathers of his wings brushed her biceps as he retracted them, sending goosebumps skittering down her arms. Then he gestured with one hand in the direction they had come, and she gave him a nod.

There was nothing left to say.

THIRTEEN

Five minutes later, she stood to one side of the bridge with Reg, Nora, and Axill. At least a dozen other former abductees were still scattered around the bridge, because, who wanted to leave on the off chance something interesting happened? Instead, Sovah's last minute instructions to Guan were kind of routine, and borderline dull.

Reg huffed. "This is ridiculous."

"Well," Nora whispered. "Stop staring at him, then."

"I'm trying, but he's so...you know." He fluttered his fingers in Guan's direction as if that explained everything.

Ava shot a skeptical look at her former cellmate. "No, what?"

"Gorgeous." Regina hand-fanned his face.

"Hm." The guy was handsome, but not in the mature, silver fox way Sovah was. "Nope. Not seeing it."

Axill made a wheezing noise in his chest that sounded like suppressed laughter. *Someone* agreed with her assessment, even if it was for different reasons.

And speaking of Axill, and by default, Nora... She gave

their clasped hands a pointed look. "I guess I missed a lot while I was off trying to save your butts."

Nora's cheeks turned pink, and she tipped her head back—way back, because Axill was at least a foot taller than her—to meet his gaze. For his part, Axill's expression softened as he raised Nora's hand and brushed his lips over her knuckles.

Watch out, Hollywood. There's a new powerhouse couple coming your way.

Hopefully, it'd last more than a few weeks. Despite his fame, Axill seemed genuinely smitten with the little librarian. What would the press call them? Axora? Norell?

All the Bezchian officers came to attention, and she dragged her focus back to Sovah. He took them all in with his gaze, as if every single one of them were important to him personally, then returned their salutes with one of his own. They knew that this could be the last time they saw him alive—it showed in their eyes. That mix of sadness for what could happen, and hope that somehow things would go well.

Sovah nodded, as if he wasn't about to face possible death, then made a sharp about-face and moved toward the doors. Toward her. She raised her chin and met his gaze as her heart lodged in her throat. Despite her inner turmoil, she'd be damned if he'd see anything less than respect and love in her expression.

Ah, what could have been.

He stopped in front of her, nearly toe-to-toe so she had to tilt her head back, much the way Nora had done moments ago. God, he was magnificent. He raised one hand and caressed her cheek with his thumb pad, warm and rough.

Who needed words when the sorrow in her heart reflected in his amber eyes?

Then he lowered his hand, turned, and stepped through the doorway. And out of her life.

Better now than after she'd really developed feelings for him. She swallowed against the hard lump rising in her throat.

Too late, you damn fool.

The *swoosh* of the doors snapping closed sounded so final, and the silence on the bridge weighed on her like a heavy blanket. In fact, it was too silent. She turned her attention away from the doors. Every set of eyes was on her, most expressing some degree of surprise or sympathy, and a couple, confusion. In all fairness, it wasn't like she and Sovah had had time to advertise their mutual attraction.

Guan cleared his throat, breaking the spell. "Yes, well, civilians, we might be in for a rough flight. You know where the crew safety seats are. Go quickly. We will depart momentarily."

There were safety seats?

"All right," Reg said in his don't-mess-with-me stage manager voice. "You heard the man, people. Let's go." In less than twenty seconds, everyone had passed them, and Reg grasped her upper arm. "Come on, Ava."

"Right."

She allowed Reg to lead her down the corridor, Nora and Axill trailing behind. Each step taking her farther from Sovah.

"Whatcha let him go for, honey?" Reg muttered the words. "I mean, I know...*we* know about your supposed crime and the Protectorship, and all the shit that this might be a suicide mission for him. But, does it *have* to be?"

"It is true," Axill rumbled behind her.

She glanced over her shoulder. "Life isn't always like the movies, Axill. Sometimes the girl doesn't get the guy and live happily ever after."

"But strong heroines, they fight for it. Sometimes they win, sometimes they do not. Who knows which it will be? The only certainty is that the ones who do not, end up bitter."

A small gasp popped out of her. What the actual fuck? How dare he presume? She jerked free of Regina's grip and whirled around to face him, a thousand words jonesing to escape. Axill lowered his chin and raised his blond eyebrows, a wordless dare for her to deny it. And she couldn't. God help her, she couldn't. She loved that damn flying man.

"Shit."

Axill nodded. "Ja. Shit."

She met each of her friend's gazes. "I'm not spending the rest of my life wondering what happened to him."

That'd be a lot of years playing the *What If* game, and Axill was right. It would turn her bitter. Robyn and the girls would understand. They had to.

Nora squeaked, bouncing up and down on her toes.

Reg pressed his hand to his heart. "I *knew* it. You love that surly silver hunk."

"He's *not* surly." Much.

"Cha, it doesn't matter, honey." Reg flailed one hand as if waving away her protest. "Thank sweet baby Jesus you came to your senses."

Axill just grinned like a benevolent Norse god, which was fitting on so many levels.

She returned his smile. "You're going to wow the Academy with your acceptance speech someday, kid. I'm sorry I'm going to miss it."

"If I continue acting, maybe." He glanced at Nora as if the center of his universe was shifting. The guy had it bad. Heck, the way Nora was looking back at him, they both did.

"What about you, Reg?" She met the drag queen's dark-eyed gaze. "Are you going to stay for that cute young man on the bridge?"

"*Young* is the operative word there, honey." Regina shrugged. "Maybe in another decade, if the bozos at the Alliance ever make contact with Earth. Still, tradition is a big deal with Guan. Have the good captain explain mate-matching to you."

A vibration rumbled through the floor under her feet, and Nora's eyes widened. "They've started the engines."

Panic surged through her. "How do I get off this piece of shit ship?"

The Night Stealth was easy, and she might be able to navigate *Axiom*'s hallways in a pinch, but she'd seen very little of the grays' cargo ship.

Axill guided Nora over to Regina. "You two go, I will get Ava to the door. Nora, save me a seat?"

"I will."

"Hurry, Ava." He grabbed her hand and trotted back the way they'd come.

"Uh." She gave Regina and Nora a final over-the-shoulder glance. Both wore ear-to-ear grins, waving their farewells. "Bye."

Several confusing turns later, a closed hatchway came into view and a muffled mechanical hum reached her ears.

"That is it." Axill frowned and quickened his pace. "Hurry. Sounds like the ramp is still retracting."

"But the door's closed."

"Who do you think opened it for the civilians against Guan's orders?" He drew her to a stop and furiously punched a sequence of buttons on the control pad next to the door.

She blinked at him. *So, not the stereotypical hunky superstar actor of very little brain, I guess.*

The door *whooshed* open, exposing the retracting ramp and a large, winged Bezchian sprinting away across the hangar floor toward a row of smoldering machinery.

"There he is!" The sudden screech of an alarm assaulted her ears, and she clapped her hands over them. "What the hell's that?"

"You have about ten seconds before someone on the bridge overrides the door controls."

Oh, is that all? "Can you stop the ramp?"

"No. You will have to jump."

"*What*?" Her breathing turned into small, panicked pants. Maybe he wasn't so bright after all. "That's fifty feet *straight down*, Axill!"

He wrapped his hand around her right biceps and guided her out onto the ramp. "But your captain can fly."

Oh. Right. Of course. Because that went so well last time. *Breathe. Stay calm.*

"Be happy, Ava."

"You too, Axill." She managed to squeak the words out. "Thank you."

He grinned. "It is nice to be a superhero in real life for a change."

The door snapped shut. And now she was alone. Outside a freaking spaceship. With a retracting ramp. She turned and froze in place, her gut twisting in a spectacular knot. Only fifteen feet of that ramp was left before she'd plunged to the floor…to her death. And Sovah had almost reached his hiding place.

Well, there was only one thing left to do. She took in a deep breath and screamed his name.

"Sooo-vaahhhhh!"

The desperate undertone of his name being shrieked from behind him twisted his heart in his chest. "*Ava.*"

He flared out his wings to slow his momentum then banked hard right. The sight of her outside the vessel at the top of the almost fully retracted ramp tore his heart. There was no way he could reach her before the ramp disappeared from under her feet and she plummeted to her death.

Save her!

He gave his wings a mighty pump to propel himself forward. "Jump, Ava!"

Her face turned paler than the white sands of the Bezchian desert.

"Trust me, viché." Her leap could close the gap between them just enough for him to catch her.

Her gaze flicked between him, the approaching end of the ramp, and back. Determination lit her eyes and her lips thinned into a flat line.

Go. Do it, love.

She ran four steps then hurtled her body over the edge, her legs and arms still moving even after she was airborne. The ear-pounding thump of his wings cutting through the air dominated his senses like a heartbeat. Loud, but not enough to drown out her terror-tinged warrior's yell, so similar to the one Rena had made the day she had flown into the storm.

I could not save my sister, but I can save Ava.

He twisted mid-air, flipping over to fly upside down. The impact of her body against his chest gave him a little wobble. He wrapped his arms around her chest and hips, locking her against him as he soared upward and away from the cargo vessel. It was an awkward position, but secure enough to get her to safety.

"Oh, my god. Oh, my god." Ava's voice cracked as she clung to his arms, her fingernails digging into his skin and her breath warm against his biceps.

"I have you, viché." He turned his face to nuzzle her hair and inhale her sweet scent. "You are safe."

Safe from falling to her death, at least. But not from the future she had chosen to face.

"I did it," she half-sobbed, half-laughed. "I jumped, and you caught me."

"Yes, and yes, love."

Why did you not stay where you were safe?

He floated down behind the bank of destroyed control equipment, the deck once again solid under his boots, and set her down gently. She turned toward him, her face alight with joy. Relief gave way to anger. How could she be happy after nearly killing herself?

He gripped her by her shoulders and bent to peer into her eyes. "*Why* did you do this? Why did you not listen?"

"Because—"

"One little thing, Ava. If one little thing had gone wrong, I would have lost you." Forever. There were no second chances with death. "All because you did not do as you were told."

And I still might lose her.

Her lips parted, and the light of understanding rose in her eyes. "You...lost someone. Didn't you? Someone you loved, who broke the rules."

How had she deduced that so quickly? He forced his mouth closed and tightened his jaw muscles. It did not matter how, she simply had.

"You were safe, going home to your family and friends." The words were nothing more than a desperate attempt at diversion.

She cupped one of her hands over his cheek. "That's why you're such a stickler for rules, isn't it?"

Immortals help him, she was far too perceptive.

"Who was it, Sovah?"

He lowered his chin toward his chest and gazed at the metal deck. "My sister, Rena. She was eight sun migrations, and I was five, the day she took a taunting dare from another youngling and tried to prove herself by flying into an oncoming fury. A storm too strong for most adults to fly in. She did not survive."

"Oh, my love." Then her arms were around him, comforting, supporting, understanding. "I am sorry. I didn't mean to hurt you. It's just, I couldn't...can't...leave you. Not with the way I feel. And trust me, Robyn and the girls will understand." A small bubble of laughter escaped her. "They'd probably be pissed if I *didn't* stay."

He pulled back far enough to see her face. "How will they feel if you die with me? Or end up incarcerated?"

"It wouldn't matter to them." She pressed her palms flat against his chest. "What they would ream me a new one for is if I was stupid enough to walk away from love."

All the words of reprimand died in his throat as he stared down at her. She *loved* him? "That...is...a good reason."

"You bet it is." She closed her hands around fistfuls of his uniform and yanked him down to her level then claimed his mouth with hers.

Joy burst over him, and he pulled her tighter to his body, deepening the kiss. Love. She loved him, enough to risk it all.

"*Captain?*" Guan's voice filtered through the fog of ardor. "*Should I redeploy the ramp?*"

He pulled back, ending the kiss and touching his forehead against Ava's. "No, Sentry Commander. Go, now, before *Axiom* arrives."

"*Yes, Captain.*"

The air in the bay warmed as the cargo vessel turned and floated toward the entrance.

He ran his tongue over his lips then released a soft sigh. "You understand that you may still have sealed your own death, right?"

"Oh, I know." She had the audacity to grin. "But we're not dying. Not today, and not anytime soon."

"You cannot be certain of this." The faint sucking sound of the cargo vessel passing through the forcefield reached his ears, then it was gone.

"Maybe not, but I can do everything in my power to make sure we live long enough for me to drive you crazy for a while."

A matching grin teased the corners of his mouth. "Maybe longer?"

"Mmm, possibly. If we get out of here soon."

"I cannot leave the bellwether, you know this." But she could, aboard the Night Stealth.

She will not agree to leaving me here.

That would invalidate all her recent actions. The idea fizzled and died before it was fully formed.

"No, Sovah, your *tracer* can't leave the bellwether…but *you* can."

He tipped his head to one side and frowned. "What—"

"Oh, for heaven's sake…use your talons to cut it out."

He let his mouth fall open. Now why had he not thought of that? "This still does not solve the problem of Protectorship Command pursuing us."

"One thing at a time, babe. We have the Night Stealth, so it'll take them a while to track us down. Plenty of time to come up with a long-term plan."

They would be fugitives, *but* they would be together. Was he really considering this insanity?

Yes. Yes, I am.

The beginning of a new and better idea niggled at him, and he pressed his lips to her forehead in a brief kiss. "Ava…"

"Hmm?"

"I love you, too, viché."

FOURTEEN

God Almighty, how had she forgotten about the whole jumping to light-drive thing?

"Are you secure and ready?" Sovah asked from the Night Stealth's captain's perch.

"Strapped in, yes." She ran her pink tongue over her lips. "Ready, no. But if I can dig into your bloody arm and yank out a hunk of off-worlder tech, I can do this. Punch it."

He gave her a nod and tapped his finger over the light-drive button.

"I'm not going to barf. I'm not going to barf. I'm not go— *ohhhmyyygodddd*!"

She squeezed her eyes closed and wrapped her fingers around the safety straps over her shoulders. And there went her stomach, relocating itself to her toes, again. Yeah, she was so going to barf.

"Ava?"

Anytime now, it was coming.

"Ava?"

"What?"

"Open your eyes, viché. The dampers are functioning fully. You are fine."

"Says you." She slowly raised her eyelids anyway. Sure enough, the geometric light designs spun on the view screen. "Hey, I didn't throw up."

Wonders never ceased.

Sovah's warm chuckle wrapped around her. "No, you did not."

The unspoken *as I said* lingered in his grin. Such a smart ass.

"Well, then." She forced her hands to unclench then lowered them to rest oh-so-casually to her lap. "You going to share the rest of your plan with me now?"

"We fly dark to Bezchi, which will take two days." He pressed a few buttons on the console in front of him then turned his perch to fully face her. "This vessel is one of the fastest in the fleet. There are two more like it, but given their current locations, they will not be able to overtake us before we arrive."

Lucky thing, that. "But won't your bosses be able to intercept us once we land?"

"They will try. But I have a contact planet-side who is rather resourceful, and highly placed in the Raptorclaw monarchy."

"Trustworthy?"

"Absolutely."

She let out a small laugh. "Pays to have friends in high places."

"It does." He retracted his safety straps, leaned forward on his perch, and started tracing lazy, swooping designs over the silk of her PJ covered thigh with one talon. All her blood rushed to her groin, and her girly bits pleaded for her to jump his bones. "If this contact can arrange it quickly enough, he will take us directly to an audience with the Raptor monarchs, Careene and Kyzel, where we can petition for asylum with my clan."

"And…." Oh lord, her voice wobbled. She swallowed hard as if that'd help her concentrate around his invisible artwork on her leg. "And if he can't arrange it?"

Sovah twitched one of his wings upward in what could've been a shrug. "He will, eventually. Our requests for such an audience legally protects us until the monarchs are available to hear our petitions. Waiting a day or two, or longer, will not matter."

Okay, that was good.

"But." He shifted even closer, fully in her personal space, which was exactly where she wanted him. "There is something that cannot wait, Ava."

Click. He undid one of her safety buckles.

She ran her tongue over suddenly dry lips. "And what thing is that, Sovah?"

Click. Another buckle fell open. "Us."

And right on cue, those nipples of hers perked right back up to say hello to him from under her PJ top.

Click.

The final buckle was out of the way. "Well, then, engage the autopilot, Captain Raptorclaw."

"Already done." Sovah scooped her off her perch like she weighed no more than a feather, and all but raced down the hallway.

Oh, yeah, baby.

Next thing she knew, she had landed on the cushy softness of a bed. Sovah's gaze smoldered. One look conveyed exactly what was on his mind, and she was completely on board. She pushed herself to her knees, grasped the hem of her PJ top and yanked it up over her head. Then she slid out of the bottoms and tossed both pieces...somewhere else. It didn't matter where.

"Ava." He whispered her name with reverence as his gaze skimmed down her body.

The thrill of being exposed to him raced up her spine. And there was no judgement in his expression, only wonder mixed with...fascination? Satisfaction?

He raised his gaze to meet hers, and blinked. "You are worried."

"Sort of." Did normal women her age get sudden-onset sex-anxiety about doing the horizontal tango with a different species? "I mean, I'm pretty sure we're compatible—"

"Stop."

Now it was her turn to blink at him.

He undid the hidden snaps down each side of his uniform shirt then lifted it slowly over his head and tossed it in the same general direction as her PJs had flown. Next, he tugged off his boots, while standing, no less. That was pretty impressive balance. Her breath hitched in her chest as he hooked his thumbs under his waistband and slowly shimmied his pants down and off. Then he stood fully upright, and fully erect in the place she was most interested in at the moment.

And suddenly, nothing else mattered. Being naked. Him seeing her old body. How different she might be from a

Bezchian woman. Her balding nether regions—something her momma had never warned her could happen as she got older.

He stroked his hand slowly down his shaft. "Compatible enough, yes?"

She reached out and traced her fingertips over the ridges that defined his abs down to the flat bed of silky, silvery feathers surrounding his cock. At least a half-dozen flesh-colored rings lined its length, and they seemed to flutter as she moved her hand closer. Now that was a potential game-changer, in a good way.

"Yes." She managed to croak out the word and nod at the same time.

Afterall, bits were bits, and her bits were hot to trot for his.

He went slowly to his knees next to the bed. "Lie back, viché. Yes, like that, but close to the bed's edge."

She scooted her butt to where he indicated, and nearly stopped breathing when he shifted his gaze to her exposed core. He ran the rounded curve of one talon over her clit, and a shudder of pure pleasure tore through her.

Obviously, Bezchian women had their most sensitive equipment located in the same places as she did. He lowered his head, and this time took her into his hot, wet mouth. A gasp of delight escaped her as she bucked her hips upward. Sovah's knowing chuckle extended the sensation then he pressed and swirled his tongue over the hyper-sensitive spot.

"Oh. My. *God.*" She grasped the tufts of headfeathers and tugged until he looked up with a big-ass grin. "We…can do that…later. Need you inside me…now."

It almost looked like he would say no, but then he was

over her, his weight securing her to the mattress as he claimed her mouth with his. Smart man. The kiss was as encompassing as the one they had shared before catching up with the bellwether. He drew her tongue into his mouth at the same moment he slammed his cock balls-deep inside her.

All semblance of sanity fled her normally well-ordered brain, and her thoughts scattered as Sovah slid back and surged forward...and those cock rings fluctuated. She broke off the kiss, gasping as he hammered into her without mercy.

"A-va," he growled next to her ear. "Take me, brand me as yours...now."

"Yes. Yours. Mine." She grunted the words in rhythm with his thrusts.

That was as much of a sentence she could make with him plunging in and out of her, tightening the coil of her impending release.

He swiveled his hips once, twice, and her universe exploded, sending her over the edge as she clamped down on his thickness. A scream of raw carnal pleasure tore from her. Sovah arched his back as his wings fully unfurled as he came. His cock rings hit all the right spots, spinning her into another mind-bending orgasm.

A moment later, the only sounds were both of them panting in the dimly lit room.

Sleep dissipated, pushing her back to the land of consciousness. And the awareness of the hard, masculine body pressed against her side.

Ah, Sovah.

The weight of his muscled arm over her belly, and the slow, warm puffs of breath fanning against her neck, felt like home. After decades of believing she'd orgasmed with other partners, what a way to discover that she really hadn't.

And at my *age!*

She curved her mouth upward into a smile like a satisfied cat who'd caught the canary. Or, as in this case, the really big, sexy owl-guy. If she'd known up front that she'd end up in bed feeling this delicious, with Sovah's soft wing pillowing her shoulders, she would've attached herself to his chest the moment she'd first smacked into him, instead of running away.

She extended her arms over her head and arched her back in a full body stretch.

Sovah nuzzled his nose deeper into her hair and audibly inhaled. "You smell like the air currents in summer."

A chuckle bubbled out of her, and she rolled onto her side to face him. "And you smell like vanilla." If she hadn't retired, she would've figured out how to capture his exact scent in a bottle. It'd be the sexiest men's cologne ever.

"Is va-nil-la a good thing?"

"Mm, the best. Better than cinnamon, even." She tilted her head back and gave the corner of his mouth a kiss. "Like you."

A teasing sparkle lit his amber eyes. "I am the best."

"Well, don't let it go to your head, but yes. In my book, you are."

"You are the best, too." The humor faded a little to something more serious. "Ava, no matter what happens after we reach Bezchi, would you consider taking me as your life-mate?"

A marriage proposal. She'd had a few of them over her lifetime, none of which she'd ever come anywhere close to accepting. But this one?

"Yes, Sovah. I will happily bind my life with yours. God knows how this happened, but I'm head over heels in love with you, sweetheart."

"And I with you, viché." Sovah brought his hand up and cradled her head in his large palm. "Shall I show you again?"

"Oh, hell, *yes*."

FIFTEEN

———————✳———————

Two days later.

The jarring buzz of the proximity alarm filled the cockpit as a freighter seemed to appear from nowhere. Sovah jerked the Night Stealth's navigation stick hard to port, swooping around the huge vessel.

"Fucking *hell*, Sovah." Ava clung to her safety restraints, her knuckles white.

Some might say careening unannounced into the raptor clan's spaceport was not one of his most brilliant ideas, but there had been little choice. Informing flight control of the Stealth's approach and requesting permission to land would have alerted Protectorship Command, giving them an opportunity to intercept. Even the stalwart Prime Advisor Rol Raptorclaw had agreed that was not a risk worth taking.

On the other wing, close calls like this were certainly not helping his mate's engrained fear of flying. That was something he would need to work with her on once her asylum was granted and she was safely ensconced in his nest.

Our nest.

He recentered the navigation stick. "My mate suggested I try *bending the rules* a little more often."

"I didn't mean the laws of physics!"

The berth Rol had assigned for them loomed ahead. "Almost there, viché. Get ready to fly."

Moments later, he had guided the Night Stealth in and powered it down. Disembarking without waiting for clearance was yet another risk. But after blasting into port the way they just had, it would not take long for the Protectorship guards to figure out where the vessel had come from and who must be flying it.

"Door override activated. Go, Ava. *Go.*" He freed himself from his restraints and followed his mate, who was already sprinting down the hallway.

She paused at the edge of the open doorway and raised her arms, her pale hair spinning wildly in the up and down drafts of the port. The disembarking gangway was not in place yet, just as he had anticipated. He plowed into her from behind, folding her into his embrace and sailing both of them across the gap toward the open doorway on the other side.

The moment his feet found purchase on the solid concourse floor, a tall, brown-winged male appeared and beckoned with one hand. "This way, Captain. We will travel by foot to avoid Protectorship guards."

Ava's breath stuttered. "I hope that's your friend."

"That is Prime Advisor Rol, yes." He slid his hand into one of hers and gave it a gentle tug. "We must hurry."

The footrace from the spaceport to the royal residence was blessedly free of incidences of conflict. Although Rol abruptly change direction twice, leading them between buildings that were not along the most direct route.

Finally, they entered the royal residence, the ground-level door swooshing closed like a sigh of relief. Ava's hand tightened around his as she tilted her head back farther and farther until her gaze reached the ceiling of the wide-open entry, seven stories above.

"Wow," she breathed.

Rol turned to them. "As I predicted, the safest route was by foot. They did take to the air in search of you. It has finally occurred to them to search the walkways between the buildings."

"We are grateful, Prime Advisor." Sovah raised his hand and touched two fingers to the point of his headfeathers.

"It was my pleasure, my friend. After all your years of stellar service representing our clan and protecting our interests, it is my honor to see to your safety and that of your mate." Rol mirrored the greeting to him, and then again to Ava. "Welcome to the Raptorclaw clan, Ava Martin."

"Thank you, Prime Advisor." Ava touched her own two fingers to the center of her forehead.

Even without headfeathers, she was flawless. He allowed a sense of pride to fill his chest.

"Captain." Rol's unique, heterochromatic eyes flicked back to him. "Protectorship Command has retaken possession of the Night Stealth."

Another anticipated action confirmed. Even so, it marked the true end of that stellar career. Poignant, yet in many ways, oddly liberating.

He gave Rol a single nod. "Thank you, Prime Advisor."

"Come, this way." Rol turned and strode toward a set of ramps switch-backing from floor to floor above them.

Normally, visitors would take wing to the landing platform of the floor they needed, yet that was not feasible given Ava's feelings about heights. But the need to stay one wing-span ahead of Protectorate Command was over. His little Earthling was safe here, and if walking to the monarchs' audience chamber made her more comfortable, so be it. It would only take a few moments longer, anyway.

Soon, they reached the fifth level and were striding along the high-polished, dark-wood hallway floor toward the audience chamber. Ava's grip around his hand tightened.

"Relax, viché." He murmured the words for her ears only.

"Easier said than done."

True. While he had every faith in the outcome of Monarch Kyzel and Careene's decision, she was leaving her fate in the hands of two strangers from another world. But, in the unlikely event his monarchs should fail them, he already had an avenue of escape in mind. There were neutral worlds that did not belong to the Galactic Alliance of Planets where they could build a new nest, together.

He gave her shoulder a playful wing-bump. "You have been through worse today, eh?"

"You mean almost getting sideswiped by that freighter?" She shuddered with exaggerated drama. "That was some creative flying, Ace."

"Hmm. How did you say it? It pays to have friends in high places?"

"No kidding." She raised her gaze to the sky-blue walls

and white ceiling. "This is like walking through the clouds on a summer day."

That was something he had not thought of in a long time. How refreshing to see his home through her eyes. "Such is the intent. Most nests reflect this sentiment."

"Including yours?"

"Yes, including *ours*."

Her gaze met his again. "I can't wait to see it."

There was a suggestive undertone to her words. However, it would not do to succumb to the urge to grab her, leap out the nearest window, and take her there now.

Swoosh.

A door ahead and to their left opened, and Rol entered. Ava's stride slowed then she came to a stop just outside the audience chamber.

"Viché?" He moved to stand in front of her.

She took in a slow, deep breath through her nose and released it through her pursed lips. "I am a flower soaking up the sun in a meadow. Calm and confident as a pristine mountain lake. This is no different than release day for a new product. I got this."

"Yes, you do." He pulled his wings forward, surrounding them, shutting them off from the rest of the world, if only for a moment. "No matter what decisions are made today, we will face them together."

"Together." She nodded and placed her hand to his cheek, her pale, soft skin warm. "You're the whipped cream on the sundae of my life, Sovah."

The what? He narrowed his eyes in speculation. "Is that good?"

"Very good." A twinkle of laughter reflected in her blue eyes. "Okay, I'm ready."

"I know." He bent close and pressed his lips to hers in a brief kiss, hoping it would impart all the love he held in his heart for her. Then he took her hand and led her through the doorway.

The audience chamber had changed very little over the years since the current ruling pair had been elected. Sunlight flooded through the wide window-doors lining the outside wall. Spacious, sparsely furnished, open to the landing and gathering balcony outside.

"Reminds me of a Mediterranean villa I stayed at once after the madness of a Fashion Week in Milan," Ava whispered.

Before he could process her words, the two Bezchians near the windows with Rol turned to face them. Yes, Kyzel and Careene had aged since his last visit, as younglings tended to do. Particularly those in leadership roles. Even though they were both mid-forty sun migrations, fine lines traced deep around their eyes and bracketed their mouths.

"My monarchs." He slipped his arm away from Ava and went down on one knee.

The accompanying joint pops seemed to echo louder than they had the last time he was here. Clearly, they were not the only ones to have aged.

Careene moved forward, her dark gray-blue headfeathers catching the sunlight and her white and gray striped wings flowing in her wake like a cape.

"Sovah, our old friend." There was a melodious tone to her voice, and she clasped her taloned hands around his shoulders. "Rise and be welcome."

"Thank you, Monarch Careene." He pushed up off the floor. "Kneeling does not come as easily as it once did."

"Then do not kneel." Careene's black-as-night eyes twinkled with undisguised delight. "You have been a life-long friend to Bezchi, our clan, and to Kyzel and me. Your comfort is our contentment."

"Agreed," Kyzel chimed in as he moved to stand shoulder-to-shoulder with his mate.

"As long as I breathe, I will honor you both. And speaking of honor…" He slipped his hand around Ava's again then raised it to his chest. "This is Ava Marie Martin of Earth, my mate who holds my heart."

Careene drew in a breath as wonder filled her gaze. "You have done the bonding ceremony, then?"

"Yes, my monarch. It was somewhat unconventional, but the rites were done via a comm as we traveled here."

Most Esteemed Elder Uri Firewing had not been thrilled by the request but had grudgingly preformed a version of the ceremony that would hold up under legal scrutiny. There were advantages to being "too old" to be mate-matched for the purpose of starting a brood.

One corner of Kyzel's mouth twitched up. "To ensure no one could separate you. A commendable strategy."

"Not a strategy, my monarch. Love."

"And the only reason I'd ever bind myself to anyone." Ava's smile widened and her face was aglow with happiness. "Took me sixty years, and a one-way trip to another planet to find this guy. But it's been worth every second."

Yes, it certainly had been. And there was not a moment

he would change, because even the difficult ones had been essential to bring them together.

The weight of an extended silence pulled his attention back to his monarchs. Both of them wore different expressions of contemplation—Kyzel's one of polite interest, and Careene's as though discovering a delightful novelty. Not surprising reactions as mating for love was unheard of on Bezchi. He and Ava did not fit the mold of Bezchian societal norms, on many levels.

And, really, that was not surprising either.

Ava dipped her head in their direction. "Thank you for the audience, Monarchs."

"Of course." Kyzel's blue-eyed gaze moved to her. "We are aware of what you did, and how that led to the capture of the grays' bellwether, Ava Martin. Thank you for that. How can our clan show its gratitude?"

Ava's throat bobbed with an audible swallow. "I...*we*...seek asylum with the raptor clan of Bezchi, Monarchs."

Careene folded her hands together in front of her. "We are already aware of Sovah's part in this matter. Please, tell us from whom you seek our protection and why?"

Ava started from the beginning, relating her abduction, running into Sovah...then running away from him. How he had provided her with the means to communicate, and his desire to help her and her friends return to Earth. The bellwether taking her friends and his crew, and Protectorship Command denying him permission to go after them.

Careene and Kyzel's attention on her never wavered as she took full responsibility for her so-called crime of abducting him and stealing the Stealth, skillfully leaving Rota out of it, and the positive outcome in the end. When she finished, she shot him an uncertain glance. He gave her a wink of reassurance, and her shoulders relaxed a fraction.

The two monarchs exchanged a knowing look then Careene waved Rol forward. "What are the ramifications of accepting Ava and Sovah's petitions, Prime Advisor?"

"Strong objections among other things from Protectorship Command, and possible penalties from the Galactic Alliance of Planets," he replied. "There is no telling how severe those penalties might be."

Kyzel pursed his lips into a thin line. "Will the Alliance expel Bezchi?"

"Not unless the monarchs from the other clans refuse to support us."

"And have they?"

"I have spoken to the monarchs of the Waterdiver, Landwalker, and Rockdweller clans, and also the Most Esteemed Elder of the Firewing clan. All have considered the situation, and all proclaimed they will support your decision, whatever that may be."

"What about Protectorship Command?" Careene asked.

"As Captain Raptorclaw's record of service protecting the citizens of the Galactic Alliance is above reproach, it is not in their best interest to publicly defeather him." Rol moved his gaze to Ava's. "I fully expect them to pursue any and all legal avenues available against Ms. Martin, as few as those may be. However, if she is under our protection, I am sure she will put the good of our clan and Bezchi above her personal needs."

"One hundred percent." Ava nodded.

Another exchange of glances and barely perceptible nods passed between the two royals then Careene turned her full attention to his mate. "Ava Martin, as the monarchs of the Raptorclaw clan, we are pleased to grant you your request for asylum, and all the protections afforded to our citizens. Furthermore, you have been granted extended amnesty from Clans Waterdiver, Landwalker, Rockdweller, and Firewing. You are free to roam and explore our lovely home world. Rol?"

"My monarch?"

"Please inform the Galactic Alliance of Planets and Protectorship Command that we will not be extraditing Captain Sovah Raptorclaw of Bezchi, nor Ava Martin, formerly of Earth."

"As you wish, my monarchs." He bowed his head with reverence, then strode from the room.

"Is there anything else, Ava Martin?" Careene asked.

"Um, no. Wait, yes. Can we talk about how to get the Alliance to make contact with Earth at some point?"

Careene grinned and took her by the hand. "First, you must join me on the balcony, and I will ply you with refreshments while you tell me about your home world. Then, we will discuss how to influence the Alliance in this matter."

There was no time for any words, only an apologetic look from Ava as Careene towed her toward one of the open doors to the landing balcony. He cupped his hands over his heart then extended them toward her.

You have my heart.

She was not in a position to return the gesture, but she did manage a hastily blown kiss over her shoulder, which sufficed.

EPILOGUE

———————✦———————

Fifteen years later.

Ava strolled into the large gathering room of the nest she shared with the love of her life, savoring the peaceful silence and the heat of the sun-warmed stone floor under her bare feet. The light fabric of her sapphire-blue, Punjab-style leggings flowed around her ankles with each step. Dust motes danced lazily in the afternoon sunlight streaming through the floor-to-ceiling windows to the landing balcony, only to swirl in a tizzy in the disturbance of her passing.

Another gorgeous day in paradise.

Bezchi *was* paradise to her—the home of her heart, even after fifteen sun migrations. *And* despite Strauss the Louse's vindictive attempts to make it a hellish prison, bless his heart. Yes, being cut off from any and all forms of contact with Earth had been a steep price to pay, but the damn old bird had had influence with the right people. Holding the threat of sanctions against Bezchi for harboring a Protectorship fugitive had been enough to keep her ass in line to protect her adopted home world.

That and the promise she'd made to Careene, Kyzel, and Rol.

Still, it would've galled Strauss if he had known how happy she was. How she'd never regretted her decision to join her life with Sovah's. And he would definitely roll in his grave now if he had any idea just how much influence she'd secretly had over the accord admitting Earth to the Galactic Alliance of Planets a decade ago.

Funny how, in a twisted way, the only person he'd made truly miserable was himself.

A shadow passed by the windows, followed by the tell-tale whisper of wings. Sovah was home. Her heartrate increased, and she redirected her gaze to the balcony beyond the windows. Her mate glided down, his massive wings coved as he landed feet first on the stone expanse outside. God Almighty, whether he was taking off, landing, or flying, the natural grace of his beautiful form still mesmerized her.

She smoothed her hands over her loose, powder-blue, sleeveless top as she turned to face the open archway to the balcony.

Sovah stepped into the room, the sunlight glinting off his snowy-white headfeathers. "Viché."

Nope, she'd never get tired of hearing the low timbre of his greetings, or the way he folded his wings behind his back as he unbuckled his flying leathers. Even Regina would have to agree that those garments looked sexy at any age.

She met him halfway across the floor, tipping her head back. The gentle brush of his lips against hers still sent her heart soaring. When they parted, there was a secretive twinkle in his eyes and a mischievous tilt to his grin.

"I guess something big happened at the royal residence today?"

"Several things." He tapped one finger against the tip of her nose. "The representatives from the Bezchian Intergalactic Trade Guild are enroute to Earth. The negotiations should start soon."

Finally.

"Ooh, talk dirty to me, Romeo." A giggle slipped out. What seventy-five-year-old woman giggled? Like a school-girl, no less?

That'd be me.

"I have barely begun, love. Soon, you will be able to heckle Rol into ordering and receiving Earth merchandise for you to your heart's content."

It was adorable all the English idioms he'd picked up from her over the sun migrations. "And we both know how much he appreciates my heckling. But, as long as I can get cinnamon, I'll pretend not to notice his eyeballs rolling."

She might not always see eye-to-eye with the raptor clan's prime advisor, but she did respect the kid. If Rol could be considered a kid now that he'd hit sixty sun migrations. The same age she'd been when she'd first arrived here.

"I still do not understand the draw of this spice for you."

"You will, once you've tried my homemade cinnamon rolls."

Cinbin would've worked in a pinch. Too bad the Bezchian equivalent of cinnamon was considered a sacred spice used strictly by the phoenixes of the Firewing clan. And sacrilege wasn't a way to win friends and influence people on any planet.

"Then I will make sure Rol places an order for you as soon as the trade agreement is ratified."

"Robyn loved them." She gave Sovah a small smile. "You know, she's almost the same age I was when the grays abducted me."

I wonder if she's still with that idiot Kevin?

Sovah cleared his throat, glanced away, then took her hand and led her toward the cushioned bench against the wall. "There is more news."

"Do tell." Was he avoiding the topic of her niece?

"Rota has put in for her retirement."

"That's *great*." She lowered herself to sit with him. "When?"

The fact that Strauss had never discovered Rota's role in "that wingless Earthling's plot" before he'd died three sun migrations ago was sweet, secret revenge.

"In eight sun migrations." He bobbled his wings from side to side. "More or less. You know Rota. When it feels right to her."

A chuckle rumbled in her chest. "Bet Protectorship Command just loves that."

And good for her keeping them on their toes.

"I, ah, also have news of our monarch Kyzel's quest for a new mate."

A bitter-sweet ache of loss pricked at her heart. If not for the sudden onset of an incurable wasting illness, Careene would've been here to welcome the first envoys from Earth.

Ah, my friend and co-conspirator, I miss you so much.

Even after a sun migration since her bestie's death.

Crap, it was hard to imagine Kyzel with anyone else. The

two co-monarchs might not have been a love match, but they had been devoted to each other, their kids, and their people. What an awful position for him to be in. To have to find a new mate and co-monarch or resign the office to which his people had entrusted him with for life. Add to that, his determination to keep his promise to Careene and mate for love this time.

"So, the Silverstar Agency came through, then?" And why was her normally relaxed husband now bouncing one of his knees up and down?

"More than you could have realized when you recommended them to him." A strange gleam lit his autumn eyes. "Kyzel has been matched with an Earth woman."

"Get. Out." No wonder Sovah seemed excited. "Does this Earth woman have a name?"

"Her name is Robyn. Martin. Donahue."

A blank numbness filled her brain like inflating Styrofoam, and she opened and closed her mouth several times before a single word squeaked out. "Robyn…?"

Sovah nodded, the corners of his mouth twitching with a barely suppressed smile.

"*My niece*, Robyn?" But what'd happened to Kevin?

Another nod, and a full-blown grin.

How was this even going to work? Would the raptor clan accept an Earthling as their co-monarch? Chrissake, what about Robyn? Would she leave her kids behind? Oh, God forbid, if things got that far, and Kyzel fell in love, he might *abdicate*. If that happened, it'd be all her fault.

"Shit on a shingle, Sovah. What have I *done*?"

To my dear readers:

Welcome to the weirdness of the Silverstar Mates series! What I mean is that I already had three Silverstar Mates books published when the idea for Ava & Sovah's story came along. Originally, I intended to bill *Fly with Me* as the fourth book. Afterall, it was the last one written. Bu-ut…this story takes place fifteen years *before* any of the others!

So, after a lot of consideration and bugging the snot out of friends for input, I finally decided to switch things up and make this book one. However, *Fly with Me* can be read either before or after reading *Above the Storm*, *Wing and a Prayer*, and *Trial by Fire*. (The original three books should be read in order, though.)

I hope you enjoy this series featuring heroes and heroines over fifty!

~Lea Kirk

*Please turn the page
to enjoy an excerpt from*

Above the Storm
Silverstar Mates

ONE

---◆---

What is a love match? Kyzel Raptorclaw stared at the projection of the mate matching application that hovered in the air over the table in front of him. A monarch should know, should understand, but this was beyond his experience.

He shifted his backend to ease the ache from sitting too long on the coved wooden perch. Careene had known—on some level, at least. And it had resonated with her enough to pluck a death-bed promise from him.

"Your next mate, Kyzel, choose her for love, not duty or tradition. Swear it."

He had so sworn. There had been no other choice. After more than thirty-seven sun migrations together as co-monarchs of the raptor clan, he could not let her soul pass into the Great Aerie in anything other than a state of peace.

It was now nearly one long sun migration of mourning and secrets since her passing.

"Are you sure you must do it this way, Kyzel?" The

question came from the male at the opposite end of the long wooden council table.

He raised his gaze to meet Rol's eyes, one gray one blue—a unique and unfortunate combination for a raptor. His childhood friend, and full-time prime advisor, understood the reasons behind his subterfuge, but had reservations. Heavens, *he* had reservations, yet he must follow through. It was a sin to disregard a deathbed vow.

"Do you know a better way to both keep my promise and fulfill the law?" Because the law for surviving monarchs was clear: a sun migration to mourn, another sun migration to find a new mate and co-ruler.

If he did not fulfill the law, he would be replaced as the elected leader of the raptor clan. In short, he would betray the confidence of his people. Yet, fulfilling his promise to Careene could very well disturb the fabric of Bezchian society. No, not could...*would*. Once the elders found out, they would protest.

It was not his intent to undermine the immortal mate-matchers of the Firewing clan, but they did not make matches for this elusive emotion called love. Their matches were made based on logic and the strengthening of the families. It was a sacred duty they performed for the four mortal clans, and they took it very seriously.

Rol shook his head, the silvery streaks through his dark headfeathers catching the light from the ceiling fixture as he did so. "I had hoped that during your time of mourning, a better air current would open to you than the services of an agency founded by an off worlder."

So did I.

He scrubbed his hands over his face. "The Silverstar Agency has an excellent reputation for love matches. Their success rate rivals that of the elders."

"The elders did well by you and Careene."

True. Both of them had had the desired strengths of character to lead their clan, and, by law, no monarch could rule alone. So, they had entered into a mating union together, provided six heirs for the Raptorclaw clan, and led their people in harmony and prosperity.

Kyzel rested his forearms on the table and let his wings droop a fraction under the weight of the truth. "As fond as we were of each other, it was never a love match. And that is what she wanted for me."

"But, does it have to be *Earth*?"

There were many other planets in the Galactic Alliance of Planets to choose from, but something about the obscure little planet appealed to him.

A chuckle rose up. "Honestly, Rol, you have already admitted several times that such a match might help *solidify* our relationship with Earth. It is largely due to your efforts that the Bezchi Intergalactic Trade Guild has finally reached out to them with a request to open negotiations."

Rol fluffed the feathers of his mighty wings and made a harrumph sound. "Only because Captain Sovah's Earthling mate would not stop beating her wings at me."

He gave an amused huff at the turn of phrase. "Ava does not have wings."

"And that's is another issue," Rol raised one finger and shook it in his direction. "Humans have no wings, or even talons."

As illustration, Rol extended and retracted the claws embedded in the tips of his fingers.

"Her lack of wings, and the presence of finger and toe nails, does not seem to have affected Sovah's feelings for her." The older couple had been a mated pair for over fifteen sun migrations, ever since Sovah had discovered and freed the human female from an illegal slave ship.

Admit it—they have something you and Careene never had.

Something the elders had refused to acknowledge. He tapped one finger against the opposite forearm. Could Careene's close friendship with the captain and his mate be why she had made her request?

"You know," Rol said tracing a design across the tabletop with one finger, "it is not too late to have the elders match you with a younger mate who could provide more heirs."

Anger swelled in his chest. He slapped his palms against the table and rose, unfurling his wings almost fully. "Again, *no*." How many times did he have to say it? "At sixty sun migrations, the last thing I need is a new brood of fledglings to chase around. I have done my duty to Bezchi in that department, Rol. Have you?"

Red colored Rol's face from pointed peak of his headfeathers down to his chin. His friend drew his wings close to his back and dipped his head in a show of submission. "I have served our clan and Bezchi by serving you and Careene, Kyzel."

Shame washed away the anger, and Kyzel blew out a gust of air. It was not Rol's fault he was unmated. "I did not mean to devalue your contribution, my friend. Forgive my words spoken in haste and frustration."

The stress of this decision must be weighing heavier on his wings than he had realized.

He shoved his fingers through his headfeathers. "I do understand the sentiment you are trying to convey, Rol. I truly do. I do not seek to disrespect the elders; they are vital for the continuation of our society. But I have done my duty to all, as did Careene. We have assured the future of our clan, and our world, with more than enough heirs. I have no desire to enter another arrangement with a younger, fertile female. Bezchi has what it needs from me. It is my turn to find a female of age with me to share what remains of my time this side of Aerie."

The final choice was up to his mate, of course—whoever she was. And rejection was always a possibility. A ripple of unease shivered through his wings as he returned his backend to the highly polished perch. This would be a quest of faith, one in which he would put his trust in others he did not know. Others not from Bezchi.

"You spoke to your heirs, then?" Rol's question broke through his thoughts.

"Yes. They are all in support of my choice." Especially the youngest three, who were not yet mate matched.

"Then by all means, submit the application now before the rest of your advisors arrive. They will be here soon."

He shifted his gaze to the projected document and tapped the fuzzy outline of the icon marked *Submit* at the bottom. The image blinked out of existence and another took its place.

Application and bio-sample accepted. The Silverstar Agency thanks you for your application. You will be contacted by an agent for an interview. Your agent's name is Ms. Nixy Vogel.

"It is done." A deep sigh slid out. "Do you still plan to make the journey to Earth with me once a match is found?"

Rol nodded. "With any luck, the Trade Guild will have progressed to the negotiations stage with the humans by then. It would give me an opportunity to sit in on a session or two."

The soft sigh of the doors opening to admit his lesser advisors, Kopa and Vyat, ended their private conversation. Kyzel waved his hand through the projection of the Silverstar confirmation and it dissipated from view.

"Greetings, my monarch." Kopa—Rol's presumed successor when his friend eventually stepped down—bowed her head in his direction.

Vyat mimicked her action, dipping his featherless head.

"Greetings, Kopa, Vyat." Kyzel inclined his head as each took a seat on the backless perches on either side of the table.

It had been the four of them since Careene's passing. An even number—which was risky if they split on a vote. That had not happened yet, but could change today depending on how well he presented the situation at hand. And if he could convince them he was not in the beginning stages of the mindlessness. Thankfully, the cognitive-stealing condition did not normally affect one of only sixty sun migrations, and there was no history of it in his lineage.

"Thank you for your attention today." He paused as they murmured the appropriate responses. "My sun migration of mourning is near an end, and I have much to tell you about our future. I request you hold your comments and questions until I have laid out my plan."

Kopa and Vyat exchanged a brief glance, then refocused their curious gazes on him. He presented them with what detail they needed from his death bed promise to Careene.

"Rest assured, my advisors, I do not make this decision lightly. After extensive research, I have determined two facts. First, though smaller and wingless, we all know that the humans of Earth are compatible with Bezchians. Second, the Silverstar Agency has a nearly perfect love-match success rate. What remains is will you support me in this endeavor?"

Silence weighed heavy in the room, which was better than he had hoped. At least neither of them had jumped off their perches to shout him down as some sort of winged abomination. Or worse, a traitor.

"My monarch." Vyat tilted his head to one side. His crown was topped with smooth, leathery red skin instead of headfeathers. "I am not unsympathetic, but do have my reservations about this plan."

Kyzel flicked his gaze to Rol and back. "You are not alone in this, Vyat. Even I have reservations. However, after nearly a full sun migration, no better plan has presented itself. Unless you have one."

"If only I did." Vyat sighed. "Still, it is my advice that you refrain from this action and have the elders find you a new mate."

"I disagree." Kopa's caramel headfeathers framed her heart-shaped face and round golden eyes. Her kind were one of the few raptors with night vision. "Our monarch has served us well. I say that he has more than earned the right to such potential happiness, as unconventional as it may seem."

A chuffing sound of disagreement rattled in Vyat's throat. "The tradition of mate matching has also served us well, for many thousands of sun migrations."

"True." Kopa nodded. "Yet, would you agree that without the support of his advisors, Monarch Kyzel will be unable to fulfill Monarch Careene's final wish?"

"I do agree."

"And that failure to not at least attempt to do so will be a sin upon his soul, which could deny him entrance into the Great Aerie?"

Vyat shifted in his seat and lowered his gaze to where his folded hands rested on the table. "Yes."

The poor bird was as conflicted as the rest of them.

Rol's huff drew Kyzel's attention back to the opposite end of the table. "As we are all aware, the Silverstar Agency has a *nearly* perfect success rate."

Kyzel gave his head a single slow nod. Where was Rol going with this flight of thought?

"Then, there is a small chance this match will fail. If it does, will you agree to turn to the elders and accept a Bezchian mate?"

That was more than fair. "Yes, I will agree to this."

"Then you have my support, my monarch."

Satisfaction flashed in Kopa's eyes as she turned to

Kyzel. "You have my approval as well, my monarch."

"Which leaves me." Vyat chuckled and made a shrugging gesture with his hands. "Despite our current even numbers, we do not seem to be in danger of a split vote. You have my support, my monarch, although I still have reservations. But the future is unwritten, and I look forward to meeting your new mate."

Kyzel dipped his head in gracious acknowledgment. "I am humbled by your support, my advisors. Rol, will you oversee announcing our plan to our clan?"

The sooner word got out, the sooner he could address his peoples' questions and concerns. It would be reassuring to have most, if not all, on his air current before Silverstar located his mate.

I hope you are right about this, Careene.

Want more out of this world love?

Hitch a ride on the Intergalactic Dating Agency's space ship to romance! Our friendly author-pilots will take you on adventures you will never forget.

Now boarding here:
RomancingTheAlien.com

About the Author

USA Today Bestselling Author Lea Kirk loves to transport her readers to other worlds with her science fiction romance books. She's the author of the award-winning Prophecy series, and the rollicking romantic Silverstar Mates series about seasoned SFR love, that's part of the Intergalactic Dating Agency series. Why? Because sexy has no expiration date!

Ms. Kirk lives in California with her wonderful hubby, their five kids (aka, the nerd herd), and a spoiled, bossy, yet somehow adorable, pup.

LeaKirk.com